"I'm sorry, Half-Pint," Chuck said. "I shouldn't have teased you. I didn't mean to make you mad. It's just that you're usually such a good-natured kid." Smiling, he added, "Forgive me?"

"I'm *not* a kid! And while we're on the subject," Shawna added, "I wish you'd quit calling me Half-Pint. I have a *name!*"

Chuck looked confused. "But I've always called you Half-Pint."

"I didn't care when I *was* a kid. But I'm not anymore. Things have changed, in case you haven't noticed," Shawna said angrily.

Chuck gave her a long, steady look. His expression was difficult to read. Shawna's heart was beating so fast that she felt short of breath. "Yes, I guess they have," he said at last. "Now, if this argument is over, let's kiss and make up, okay?" He bent his head and brushed her lips with a quick kiss. It was just a token of friendship, nothing more, but Shawna felt as if she might actually faint.

Bantam Sweet Dreams romances
Ask your bookseller for the books you have missed

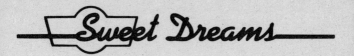

PARTNERS
IN LOVE

Susan Kirby

BANTAM BOOKS
NEW YORK • TORONTO • LONDON • SYDNEY • AUCKLAND

RL 6, age 11 and up

PARTNERS IN LOVE
A Bantam Book / January 1993

Cover photo by Pat Hill.

ISBN 0-553-29460-1

Published simultaneously in the United States and Canada

*Bantam Books are published by Bantam Books, a division
of Bantam Doubleday Dell Publishing Group, Inc. Its trademark, consisting of the words "Bantam Books" and the por-
trayal of a rooster, is Registered in U.S. Patent and
Trademark Office and in other countries. Marca Registrada.
Bantam Books, 666 Fifth Avenue, New York, New York
10103.*

PRINTED IN THE UNITED STATES OF AMERICA

OPM   0 9 8 7 6 5 4 3 2 1

Chapter One

"Shawna! I was hoping I'd find you," Chuck McCurdy said. As he got out of his vintage Mustang, the November wind ruffled his sleek, dark hair.

The red paint was so bright that Shawna Cayley shaded her eyes. "So you finally painted that thing! I was beginning to wonder if you'd ever get it done."

"Finished it just in time for the holiday dance," Chuck told her. "Are you going?"

Shawna's mouth went dry. Was he going to ask her to be his date?

"Hop in. I'll give you a lift," Chuck said, before she could reply.

He helped her into the car, and there was a thrilling warmth in his eyes as he piled red

1

roses into her lap. Shawna had never seen anything more lovely. "Are these for me?" she whispered as she breathed in the sweet fragrance.

Chuck laughed and tweaked her nose. "Go ahead and take one, Half-Pint. But the rest are for the girl I'm taking to the dance. Here she comes now! Isn't she pretty?"

Shawna strained to see who the lucky girl was. Her long, flowing hair hid her face, but when she brushed it back, Shawna saw that it was Courtney Scott, her best friend!

Pain pierced Shawna's heart. The car that had seemed so beautiful only a moment ago suddenly turned into a metal trap, shrinking and closing in on her. She was being crushed, suffocated. . . .

Shawna let out a cry of alarm and sat bolt upright in bed. Thank goodness it had only been a dream!

Just a silly dream, she thought, smiling in relief. Her older brother's friend Chuck wasn't in love with Courtney, and Courtney was head over heels for Brandon Ralston. He was the captain of the basketball team and she was a cheerleader. They were Woodrow Wilson High's perfect couple.

Shawna tiptoed across the cold floor to the window, noticing that last night's sleet made the grass glitter. She padded down the hall into her mother's second floor studio. A fresh canvas on the easel was turned to catch the morning light.

Her mother smiled at Shawna. Petite like her daughter, she was almost engulfed by her paint-smudged denim smock. "It's awfully early, honey. Did Dad wake you to say good-bye?"

"No. I had a bad dream." Shawna shivered at the memory.

"Want to talk about it?"

Shawna shook her head and reached for a blanket her mother had woven. The colorful pattern radiated warmth, and Shawna snuggled into it. "So Dad already left?"

Her mother nodded. "He had a long list of contacts. He's hoping to make it home for Thanksgiving, though, and that's only two weeks away."

Shawna's father was an inventor. When he was off on one of his trips, her mother lost herself in her art. The house always seemed quiet to Shawna without her father around.

Her older brother Gene was hardly ever home. He divided most of his time between basketball and the broken-down Mustang in the garage. He and Chuck intended to sell it, but they had to get it running first. So far, they'd spent over three hundred dollars on parts.

As Shawna watched her mother paint, her

thoughts drifted back to Chuck. She had known him for years, but recently her feelings had changed. Her palms turned sweaty when he was around and her heartbeat quickened. But to Chuck, she would always just be Gene's kid sister.

Shawna observed how her mother's brush strokes created an impression of the scene she was painting.

An impression. Was that what Shawna needed to do? Create an impression of what she wanted Chuck to see in her? It was such an exciting idea that Shawna sprang right out of her chair. For this, she'd need Courtney's help!

"What is it, Shawna?" Mrs. Cayley asked, startled by her sudden movement.

Shawna grinned. "Hunger pains," she said, thinking fast. "Can I bring you something?"

Her mother declined the offer and returned to her painting.

After Shawna wolfed down a granola bar and a glass of apple juice, she pulled on a pair of faded jeans, her southwestern print shirt, and hard-soled beaded moccasins. She brushed her shoulder-length hair until it shimmered with highlights of red and gold, then secured it at the nape of her neck with a leather tie.

Shawna grabbed her soft blue duffel coat

and hurried into the hall where she nearly collided with her brother. Gene had just gotten out of bed. He was wearing his favorite cutoff sweatpants and a rumpled T-shirt. "Where are you off to so early, Squirt?" he asked as he stretched his tall, lanky frame and scratched his blond head.

"Courtney's. There's nothing to do around here. Dad's gone and Mom's painting."

Gene yawned. "So what's for breakfast?"

"Whatever you fix, I guess. I'm out of here."

Shawna tried to sidestep him, but Gene planted a hand against the wall on either side of her, blocking her way. He grinned down at her. "You wouldn't go off and leave your poor brother to starve, would you?"

"Come on, Gene, let me go. I've got stuff to do," Shawna protested.

"Right. Like fixing my breakfast!" Laughing, he pulled her into the kitchen. "Bacon and eggs will be fine. And toast—at least six pieces, please." When Shawna still resisted, Gene said, "How about if we fix it together? I'll get the skillet."

Shawna gave up. "Okay. Get the bacon, too, while you're at it, and the eggs."

"Hey, how come I'm doing all the work?" Gene said, giving her a poke.

"Because you're a chump, that's why!" Shawna joked, grinning.

5

Gene lunged at her. "I'll get you for that!"

A knock at the back door interrupted their good-natured bickering.

"I'll get it," Shawna offered.

"And run off without fixing my breakfast? No way!" Gene loped to the door and flung it open to find Chuck standing there, his brown eyes twinkling. "What's going on?" he asked as he stepped inside.

"Shawna's fixing my breakfast," Gene said. He grabbed Shawna and hustled her over to the stove. "Pretty soon she'll be begging me to let her make lunch, too."

"In your dreams!" Shawna laughed as she broke free.

"My money's on Half-Pint," Chuck said with a grin. "She's a pretty stubborn little kid."

Chuck's sentence made Shawna stop short in her tracks. She thought of all the times he'd seen her and Gene horsing around like this, and how childish they must look to Chuck.

Trying to sound sensible and mature, she said, "Okay, Gene, let's make a deal. I'll fix cinnamon toast and pour some juice. If you want bacon and eggs, you're on your own. Want some toast and juice, Chuck?"

Chuck shook his head. "No, thanks. I thought I'd grab a bite downtown. We have to take that fuel pump back and get one that fits." He turned to Gene. "When'll you be ready to go?"

"Give me ten minutes while I shower and get dressed. Forget the toast, Squirt—I'll eat downtown with Chuck." Gene sped off, leaving Shawna and Chuck alone.

"Did you go to the game last night?" she asked.

Chuck nodded. "The Rockets won in a double-overtime. Your brother sank a three-pointer just as the clock ran out. It was a pretty exciting game."

Shawna rolled her eyes. "I should have known. If we'd lost, he'd be growling like a grizzly bear."

Chuck laughed. "How come you weren't at the game?" he asked, unzipping his leather jacket.

"I was baby-sitting for the Bradley boys next door."

Chuck was sympathetic. "All three of them? Poor kid!"

Shawna felt herself withdraw a bit. Why did he always have to call her things like "kid" and "Half-Pint"? "It's not the easiest cash I ever earned," she said. "But Christmas is just around the corner, and I need the money."

"I hear you." Chuck said with a sigh. "We're hoping to make some bucks when we sell the car. That is, if we ever get it finished."

"Why don't you check out the Burger Barn?" Shawna suggested. "I saw a help-wanted sign in the window."

7

Shawna doubted the boys would make much profit off their old car. Even though they had it running again, it still needed bodywork, the fuel pump, and a fresh coat of paint. Just as she was going to ask Chuck about that, Gene walked in.

"All set," he said, shaking his damp hair.

Shawna picked up her coat and followed her brother and Chuck to the door. "How about giving me a lift to Courtney's house?"

"I don't know, Sis. Chuck's got a two-ton limit on that old truck of his. Big thing like you might flatten all the tires," Gene teased.

"I was talking to *Chuck*," Shawna said huffily.

Chuck wrapped an arm around Shawna's shoulders, and instantly she forgot Gene's teasing. "Let's give her a ride. She's okay."

They trooped outside together, and Gene gave Shawna a boost into the front seat. The truck rode kind of rough and every time they turned a corner, Chuck's arm brushed against hers. The brief contact made her feel all hot and quivery inside, but she tried to act naturally.

"I hear you guys won last night," she said to Gene. It was all the encouragement he needed. He gave her a play-by-play account of the game until they reached Courtney's house.

Chuck got out first. "Watch your step there. It's icy," he warned. When Shawna hesitated, he put his hands on her waist and swung her lightly to the ground. His touch warmed Shawna, and with a racing heart, she smiled and thanked him for the ride.

"No problem. Catch you later, Half-Pint."

Shawna watched them drive away, wishing she had curvier curves, legs as long as a fashion model's and the elegance to match.

Chapter Two

"**S**hawna! I was just about to call you." Pert, dark-haired Courtney swung the door open and pulled Shawna into the silent house.

"Where is everybody?" Shawna asked.

"Gone. What luck, huh?" Courtney grinned mischievously. She was wearing a long-sleeved black leotard, a short diamond-print skirt, and fluorescent orange rollerblades.

"Check this out!" Courtney skated in a weaving path around the living room furniture. The Scotts' house always looked like a photo right out of *House Beautiful*. Shawna knew Mrs. Scott would never have allowed indoor skating if she had been home.

"How am I doing?" Courtney called, her cheeks flushed.

Shawna found it hard to believe that Courtney had bought the blades only two days ago. "If you weren't my best friend, I'd almost be jealous of you."

Courtney's dark eyes reflected genuine surprise. "Jealous? Of what?"

"Nothing's ever hard for you, Court. Athletics, schoolwork, boys—you just breeze through it all."

"Says the girl who after only six weeks in Mr. Harley's Business Economics class was recommended for Independent Study next semester," Courtney scoffed.

"That's nothing," Shawna said glumly.

"Nothing?" Courtney echoed. "There isn't a doubt in my mind that in a few years you'll be the most successful businesswoman earning at least eight figures, while I'm still going to be skating figure eights!"

Shawna didn't even smile.

Courtney frowned. "Since when do you need a confidence booster? What's the matter?" she asked, concerned.

Shawna was usually confident with herself, but her dream had left her troubled. She pulled off her coat, and proceeded to open up to Courtney.

". . . And then you flew into his arms," Shawna moaned.

"I would *never* do such a thing, even if

there was no Brandon Ralston in my life," Courtney stated emphatically.

"I know. I've been telling myself that since I woke up."

"So what's *really* bothering you?"

Shawna sighed. "Chuck treats me like a little kid!" Remembering the art of "impression" that had come to her that morning while she was watching her mother paint, she told Courtney what she had been thinking. "Do you see what I mean?" she concluded. "I'm not a Half-Pint—I'm a full sixteen ounces. But how do I make that impression on Chuck?"

"Try the direct approach," Courtney said promptly. "Tell him you think he's cute, handsome, adorable!"

Shawna gasped. "I could never say that!"

"Why? What's wrong with being honest?" Courtney challenged. "My brothers like it when girls tell them stuff like that."

Shawna protested. "But they're in college! The girls they date are gorgeous. What do they have to lose by being honest?"

Courtney shrugged. "Okay. If you don't like that idea, then all I can say is just be yourself."

Shawna burrowed deeper into her corner of the sofa and moaned, "Some help you are!"

"You're welcome." Courtney plunked down

beside Shawna and began to take off her skates.

"I'm only two years younger than Chuck is," Shawna said. "And even if I haven't gotten any taller since sixth grade, I've developed *some* curves. How come he hasn't noticed?"

"Maybe he just hasn't been paying attention," Courtney said. "Of course, there are ways of *making* him notice, like maybe changing the way you dress. Let's go upstairs and get started!"

In no time, clothes, scarves, jewelry, and accessories were strewn all over Courtney's room. "How about trading in all that southwestern stuff for something like this?" she asked, holding an olive-green dress up to Shawna, who made a face. It did have a certain understated style and it probably would make her look older, but she didn't like the color.

"Try it on," Courtney urged. "It'd show off your figure perfectly. As for shoes . . ."

She had just crawled into her closet when the doorbell rang.

"Want me to answer the door?" Shawna asked.

"Would you? It's probably one of my kid brother's friends. Just tell him he's not here."

But it was a man, not a child, at the door.

"Is this the Edwin Scott residence? Forty-nine West Pine?" he asked.

Shawna nodded. The man shoved a clipboard under her nose. "Delivery for Mr. Scott. Sign here, please."

"I'm just visiting Mr. Scott's daughter," Shawna said. "She's upstairs. I'll get her."

"I'm on a tight schedule. All I need is a signature, anybody's, for proof of delivery." The man pushed the pen into Shawna's hand. "Where should we unload?" he asked when she had signed.

"I'm sorry, I'm not sure . . ." Shawna said, flustered.

The man made his own decision. "The driveway, I guess." He turned away, closing the door behind him.

Shawna ran upstairs and found Courtney sitting on the floor surrounded by dozens of shoes. "Who was it?" she asked.

"A delivery man. He had something for your father. He said he'd leave it on the driveway."

"Fine." Courtney turned her attention back to the shoes and held out a pair of very high-heeled pumps. "How about something like this? They're a little awkward until you get used to them, but they do great things for your legs."

An hour passed as the girls deliberated over shoes, clothes, hairstyles, and makeup. At last Shawna stood in front of Courtney's full-length mirror, regarding her reflection critically. The snug-fitting navy blue ballet top had a scoop neckline and three-quarter-length sleeves. Navy tights under a tight miniskirt emphasized the slender shapeliness of her legs.

Courtney peeked over her shoulder, and their eyes met in the mirror. "You look great!" she exclaimed.

Shawna beamed, and gave her friend a hug. "Thanks for all your help, Court. I feel a lot better."

Together, the girls put the bedroom back in order. Then Shawna looked at the clock. "It's nearly lunchtime—I guess I'd better leave. Gene and Chuck should be back by now."

"Promise you'll call me later and tell me how Chuck reacts to the 'new you,' " Courtney said.

"Promise," Shawna agreed. She put the clothes she'd worn to Courtney's in a shopping bag and pulled on her coat.

But just outside the front door, Shawna stopped short. Rows and rows of pine trees wrapped in green mesh covered the Scotts' driveway and half of the lawn. The place looked like a forest!

"*Courtney!*" Shawna yelled as she dashed back inside. "Come out here. Quick!"

Courtney dashed out the door. "Oh no! They're the Christmas trees that must be for the Boy Scout troop." Courtney frowned. "But they shouldn't have been delivered here. Dad isn't even the scoutmaster anymore."

Shawna chewed her bottom lip. "Is your dad going to be angry?"

"He shouldn't be. I mean, it isn't *our* fault. Anyway, it's no big deal. Whoever took Dad's place will just have to come and get the trees. You can go home," Courtney said. "And don't worry about this. You're supposed to be concentrating on impressing Chuck, remember? Oh, and one more thing —the guy reads *Mechanics Illustrated*, not minds. You don't have to come straight out with it, but you could at least drop a few hints about how you feel. You know, feminine wiles?"

Shawna wrinkled her nose. "That's so phony!"

"Phony or not, it gets their attention. Look at Melissa Doty."

Shawna knew she had a point. When Melissa Doty swept through the halls of Woodrow Wilson High, heads turned. She had only to flash her dimples, flutter her lashes and smile and guys practically fell at her feet.

On the way home, Shawna practiced fluttering her eyelashes, then gave up, giggling self-consciously. A few blocks farther on, she glanced at her reflection in the shining plate

16

glass of Murphy's Bakery. Perhaps the clothes and makeup would be enough. She'd also concentrate on establishing a more mature relationship with Gene.

By the time Shawna arrived home, a few red-gold tendrils had fallen from the hairdo Courtney had created, softening the style. *Is the bright red lip gloss maybe too much?* Shawna wondered, checking her reflection in her bedroom mirror. She blotted it, then touched up her mascara. On impulse, she reached for her favorite perfume, and sprayed herself liberally. Perfect! Having spotted Chuck's truck on the driveway, Shawna knew she'd find him in the garage.

It was a multipurpose addition to the house. Her father spent endless hours there building, testing, and perfecting his inventions, most of which had to do with cooking gadgetry. One of his earliest inventions, a prototype of a gas barbecue grill, occupied one corner. It had an exhaust fan so barbecuing could be done indoors all winter long. There was also a machine that inhaled ground beef and spat out symmetrical patties ready to be cooked, and an electric device that could turn a potato into one long curl in less time than it took to sneeze, along with a huge vat to heat the oil in which the potato curls could be fried.

There was no wall to partition off Mr. Cayley's "laboratory" from the rest of the garage. Gene had his own workbench, his own tools, and his own cluttered work area. He and Chuck were restoring the Mustang in this space, and that was where Shawna found them, their heads hidden by the raised hood of the car. Butterflies swarmed in Shawna's stomach as she strolled around to the front. "How's it coming?" she asked, pretending to be interested in their project.

"So far, so good," Chuck said, without looking up.

Gene lifted his head and sniffed. "What's that smell? Mom hasn't boiled her potpourri dry again, has she?"

"That's my *perfume,* you jer . . ." Shawna caught herself just in time. She saw Gene grin and braced herself for more teasing.

"I've never seen you in that skirt before," he said, looking her up and down. "Fact is, I didn't know you owned a skirt."

"Just something I pulled out of the closet," Shawna murmured casually. They didn't have to know it was Courtney's closet.

"So what's the occasion? Or did you get all dressed up just for us?" Gene asked, his grin broadening.

"Courtney's going to call in a little while. We might go somewhere," she fibbed.

"Well, you better wash your face first. You look like you fell on Mom's paint palette." Gene chortled at his own joke.

Shawna flushed as her confidence wavered, but she refused to let it show. Instead she picked up a rag and rubbed a smudge of grease off her brother's chin. "You're pretty, too, Gene." She smiled sweetly.

Chuck glanced up then and said, "Hand me that half-inch wrench, pretty boy." He didn't pay attention to Shawna at all. *What a waste,* she thought gloomily.

Just then she heard the phone ringing. "That must be Courtney now," Shawna said, relieved to have an excuse to escape. "See you guys later."

It *was* Courtney, and she sounded frantic. "Shawna, you've got to help me!" she wailed. "When Daddy came home and found all those trees, he made a call, thinking the current scoutmaster would get rid of them. But guess what? There's *no troop*! It disbanded last summer!"

"So who ordered the trees?" Shawna asked.

"It was a mix-up. They had a standing order with this outfit in Wisconsin, and no one remembered to cancel it. And since Daddy was the last leader, it's up to him to take care of it."

"Can't he send them back?"

"No! He already called and asked. And now he's got this new idea. But it's *basketball season,* for crying out loud. I don't have any free time! What am I going to do?"

"Court, you're babbling," Shawna said.

"Why shouldn't I?" Courtney moaned. "You know my father! If he makes up his mind that something is good for me, you can bet—"

"*What* is good for you?" Shawna interrupted. "What are you talking about?"

"Selling those darned Christmas trees! Haven't you been listening?"

"What do you want me to do?" Shawna asked.

"I don't know. Something. Anything! After all, it *was* you who signed for the dumb things!"

Shawna wasn't offended. She knew when Courtney calmed down, she'd realize how unfair it was to blame her. But for now she needed to think of a practical solution.

But for the life of her, Shawna couldn't come up with one. "Don't panic, Court. I'll think of something. And as soon as I do, I'll call you back," Shawna reassured her friend.

Chapter Three

Shawna pondered Courtney's problem while she prepared lunch and set four places at the kitchen table. The delicious aroma of baking pizza bread soon lured Gene into the kitchen.

"Is Chuck staying?" Shawna asked hopefully.

"He already went home to eat." Gene looked up from washing his hands. He gave her a searching glance, then grinned. "Cheer up. He'll probably be back this afternoon."

"Makes no difference to me," Shawna claimed, though she was disappointed.

"Then why'd you go to all this trouble?" Gene asked and indicated the neatly set table.

21

"Courtney's got a problem. I'm trying to help her think of a solution, and my brain always works best when my hands are busy," Shawna said, taking the bread out of the oven.

"You have a brain?" Gene joked. Then his expression softened. He draped an affectionate arm around her shoulders. "Hey, if you like Chuck, your secret's safe with me, Squirt. But I gotta warn you, Melissa Doty's been hanging around his locker lately."

"Hi, kids," Mrs. Cayley interrupted as she walked into the room. "This looks beautiful. Let's sit down."

"Melissa's stiff competition," Gene continued. "It's okay to be jealous."

"Jealous? Me? Jealous of what?" Shawna retorted.

"Oh, Melissa's long legs. Her red hair. Her dimples. She's a knockout. Maybe I'll do you a favor and make Melissa forget all about Chuck."

"Do me an even bigger favor. Velcro yourself to the nearest dart board!" Shawna snapped.

"Velcro myself?" Gene laughed. "That's pretty good, Squirt."

"And don't call me Squirt!" Shawna yelled.

Mrs. Cayley frowned at them both. "Shawna, lower your voice. Gene, leave your sister alone."

Melissa's name wasn't mentioned again,

22

nor was Chuck's. Right after lunch, Gene left for basketball practice and Mrs. Cayley went back up to her studio. Shawna sat glumly in her room, mulling over the unhappy prospect of Chuck falling for Melissa. Gene was right. Melissa had a lot going for her, including every boy at Woodrow Wilson High.

Well, drastic solutions called for drastic measures. She'd just have to start taking instructions from Melissa. She'd flirt, flutter her eyelashes, simper and coo, even if she felt like an idiot.

The sound of Chuck's truck pulling into the driveway sent Shawna running to the window. With Gene gone, Chuck would be working on the car all alone. Her stomach fluttered as she hurried to her mirror to freshen her lipstick.

"Go for it!" she muttered to her reflection. Then she turned away before her courage fled, and wobbled purposefully to the garage in Courtney's high heels.

She found Chuck pouring fuel into the space heater. He turned at the sound of footsteps. "Are you still here? I thought you and Courtney had plans."

"She called. She's on thin ice with her father at the moment, so we're not going anywhere." *Doesn't he notice how different I look? Why isn't he saying anything?* Shawna wondered.

"Too bad." He screwed the cap on the fuel

can, then fiddled with the heater. "Since you're here, how about helping me?" he asked after a moment.

"Uh—sure. What do you need?"

"A pair of pliers. I want to adjust this heat regulator, but the knob's gone."

Shawna crossed to the workbench where tools were strewn about. It seemed to her as if Courtney's shoes were incredibly loud. She clip-clopped back to Chuck and gave him the pliers.

"Thanks." He adjusted the heat flow, slid the pliers into the hip pocket of his jeans, then opened the hood of the Mustang.

"Climb in and turn the motor over, will you, Half-Pint?"

Gritting her teeth at the childish nickname, Shawna slid behind the steering wheel and turned the key. The engine started to throb. She climbed out and watched Chuck make some adjustments.

"I could use a screwdriver, too. And a five-sixteenths-inch wrench," he mumbled.

Shawna went back to the workbench and not knowing which size was which grabbed the first screwdriver and wrench she found. Chuck took them without saying a word. His full attention was focused on the job before him. Gazing down at him, Shawna thought he had the blackest, most beautiful hair she'd ever seen.

Suddenly he turned and caught her staring. Quickly, she averted her eyes, remembering to flutter her lashes.

"Got something in your eye?" Chuck asked.

A scene from an old black-and-white movie flashed through Shawna's mind. She batted her lashes even faster. "A cinder, I think."

He smiled. "From an oil heater? I doubt it."

Heat crept up her neck. "Well, then maybe it's an eyelash. Do you think you can get it out?"

Shawna's skin tingled as he firmly clamped her chin between his thumb and forefinger and tilted her face upward. Any minute now, his gaze would darken and entangle with hers. Shawna's heart pounded as she waited for the magic moment. . . .

"I don't see a thing," Chuck said cheerfully. "You must have blinked it out."

"I guess. It's feeling much better now," she said, sighing. What was she doing wrong? He didn't even *notice* she was flirting!

Chuck continued to work on the car. The silence lengthened, and he seemed to have forgotten that Shawna was even there. Summoning up her courage, she moved a little closer and leaned against the fender of the old Mustang, trailing a polished fingernail along the dull surface.

"I had a dream about this car."

25

Chuck glanced up at her. "Really? What'd you dream?"

"That you painted it red."

He smiled. "Hey, that's good. *The Red Pony*." At her puzzled expression, he added, "Mustang? Red Pony? Remember the story by John Steinbeck?"

"Oh. As in American Lit." Shawna returned his smile.

"Was I in it? Your dream, I mean," he added.

Shawna tried out a Mona Lisa smile and lowered her lashes. "Actually, you were. You were taking Courtney to the holiday dance."

His eyes sparkled with amusement. "Interesting prospect. How'd it end?"

"The car exploded, and you and Courtney were nuked beyond recognition!" she said, miffed at his reply.

He laughed. "Thanks for the warning. I'll steer clear of red cars *and* Courtney from now on."

Shawna gave up being subtle and asked straight out, "What about the dance? Are you going?"

"I might. You want to hand me that trouble light?" He indicated a light bulb dangling from the end of a long cord. Shawna picked it up and thrust it at him, and he hung it from the hood latch.

But Shawna wanted to stay on a more interesting subject—the holiday dance. "Who will you take? Anyone I know?" she asked boldly.

He shot her a distracted grin. "What is this—twenty questions?"

"No. At last count it was only four."

"If you really want to know, I'm thinking of asking Melissa Doty. Satisfied?"

Shawna's heart sank and she made a face, hoping Chuck didn't see it. He pawed through the tools on the bench, then went to work again. For a long time, neither of them said a word.

Chuck muttered, at last. "Do you think you could help me bleed the brakes?"

Shawna smoothed her skirt with her hands. "I'm not really *dressed* for bleeding." Maybe he'd notice her now.

"Nothing messy about it. I'll tell you what to do, but I've got to elevate the front end first." Chuck opened the garage door and backed up the car, then climbed out and positioned a pair of wooden ramps in line with the front wheels.

"Ready?" Chuck asked, opening the car door.

Shawna settled herself in the seat. "What do I do?"

"Press the brake pedal when I tell you to. Don't pump it, just apply steady pressure." Chuck dropped down onto the creeper and slid underneath the car, taking the trouble light with him. A moment later, he called,

27

"Ready? *Press!* That's it. Some more—again! Once more. Okay, hold it down. Don't let up."

The high heels were awkward footwear for such a chore. Shawna held the brake so long that her leg began to ache. She bit her bottom lip and grimaced. "Are you about finished?"

Before he had a chance to answer, her foot slipped off the brake pedal. He groaned. "You have to hold it until I say let go. Ready? Let's try it again."

"I'd like to see *you* try holding the stupid pedal down in a tight skirt and these shoes!" Shawna retorted, annoyed.

"Why didn't you say something? I'll wait while you go change."

Shawna climbed out of the car and slammed the door. "It'll be a real long wait, Mr. Goodwrench!" she said angrily, heading out of the garage. "Bleed your own brakes. I've had it!"

In her haste to leave, Shawna slid on a patch of ice right outside the garage door. Chuck quickly caught her. He turned her around to face him, his expression puzzled.

"I don't get it. What are you so steamed about?"

Looking into his eyes, Shawna felt defensive, hurt, angry, and confused. She was afraid that if she tried to speak, she'd burst into tears. But he wasn't going to let go until she gave him an answer, so she said the first thing that came to mind.

"It's this money-making scheme of yours. You and Gene keep working on this car with no end in sight. You've spent three hundred dollars in parts so far, and that's just under the hood."

He blinked. "How do you know how much we've spent?"

"Never mind how I know. The point is, you're pouring a lot of money into this car with no guarantee of getting any of it back. Look at the body. If you take it to a shop, it's going to cost you a fortune to have it painted. You'll have to sell it for a lot of money if you're going to make any profit."

"I know that. But the car will be worth it."

"It's worth only as much as a buyer is willing to pay. Until then, it's worth nothing," Shawna argued. "Face it, you and Gene may not even break even on this deal. You'd both be better off with part-time jobs you can fit into your schedules."

A slow flush colored Chuck's face, and he set his jaw in a hard line. "It's not easy to find a job that won't conflict with school activities."

"I know. But you can't convince me this car is any kind of solution. What you need is something short-term," she added, "something you can get in and out of with a nice fat profit."

"Like what?" he challenged.

Shawna paused to give her whirling thoughts time to catch up with her runaway mouth. Suddenly Courtney's problem and Chuck's problem converged.

"I've got it!" Shawna cried, triumphantly. "It's perfect!"

"What?" Chuck asked cautiously.

"You can sell Christmas trees!"

Chapter Four

"*Christmas trees?*" Chuck echoed. "Where would we get Christmas trees?"

"Getting them is no problem—" Shawna began.

He cut her short. "Where the heck did you get an idea like that? I know! It's Business Economics, isn't it? I took Mr. Harley's class a couple of years ago. He was always telling us to latch on to unique business opportunities. Something he said gave you the idea, right?"

"You're not even close." Shawna told him about the trees at Courtney's house.

"I have a feeling there's a lot more to selling trees than you think, Half-Pint. Besides, I'm working on the car now, and I always like to finish projects that I start," Chuck said.

Christmas trees practically sold them-selves. How hard could it be? But there was nothing to be gained by arguing. If Shawna wanted Chuck to give the idea a fair chance, she'd have to wait until he was in a more receptive mood.

So Shawna went inside to share her idea with Courtney.

"What did the guys say?" Courtney asked anxiously from the other end of the phone.

"Well, Chuck wasn't very enthusiastic," Shawna admitted. "I haven't asked Gene yet."

Courtney moaned. "You've got to talk them into it, Shawna. I don't know what I'll do if I get stuck with the job!"

"Take it easy. I'm planning a strategy right now, and I need your help."

"Anything! Just get me out of this mess."

"Talk to your dad. Find out what the trees cost and ask him to list other possible expenses. Once I have a fair idea of the over-head, I can figure out the profit margin and give the guys the hard sell."

"But if Chuck isn't interested . . ."

"He might come around. And if he doesn't, maybe Gene and I can do it without him."

"You would? You'd do that for me? Shawna, you're the best friend in the whole world!"

"No big deal. Talk to your dad, okay?" Shawna reminded her.

After she hung up the phone, Shawna changed into jeans, a sweatshirt, and her favorite old moccasins. She uncoiled her hair and brushed it out. The girl who looked back at her from the mirror wasn't glamorous at all, and she was wearing the imprint of Chuck's greasy thumb on her chin. If Chuck didn't like the *real* Shawna Cayley, then she'd just have to get him out of her system.

Shawna returned to the garage and slid under the car, scooting along on her back until she and Chuck were side by side. He looked over at her from where he lay on the creeper.

"What's up?" he asked.

"Just thought I'd see how you're doing."

The glow of the trouble light illuminated Chuck's face. His nose and one cheek were streaked with grease, and his hands were filthy, but Shawna thought he looked more gorgeous than ever.

"If you want to bleed those brakes now, I'm ready," she said. "Show me what you're doing under here. Then maybe I'll understand my part in it."

"That makes sense. See, this is the brake line." He touched a thin black hose. "There's air in the line. When you push the brakes, it forces the air out. Then I tighten this caplike thing here. We keep doing it until the air is all out."

"That seems simple enough." Shawna

crab-crawled out from beneath the car and got behind the wheel again.

The job was nearly done when Gene came back from basketball practice, letting in a gust of icy wind. He forced the door shut and went over to stand in front of the heater, pulling off his woolen cap and gloves. "I can't believe how cold it's gotten. Feels like Christmas out there."

Shawna took advantage of the opening. "A lot of people buy their trees right after Thanksgiving."

Chuck crawled out from beneath the car. "Your sister thinks we should sell Christmas trees. That's what she's leading up to, right, Half-Pint?" He grinned at her.

Gene snorted. "Like we have time for that. And even if we did, where would we get the trees?"

Shawna immediately told him, but when she finished, he sided with Chuck. "We'll soon have this car ready to sell. Once we find a buyer, we won't have to worry about cash flow for a long time."

Shawna hid her disappointment and shrugged. "Then maybe I'll just do it myself. And when I'm rolling in dough, just remember, you had your chance!"

As Shawna trudged disconsolately back to the house, she realized that in spite of what she had said about selling the trees on her own, there was no way she could do it without the boys. There had to be some way of talking them into it. But how?

Courtney called back that night with the information Shawna had requested. Even after subtracting the initial cost of the trees, if they sold them all they would make a sizable profit. They could split the proceeds three ways and do very well. But she still had to convince the guys.

Shawna was still working on that problem the next afternoon when Gene and Chuck invited her to take a test ride with them in the Mustang. Chuck drove and Gene sat on the passenger's side while Shawna had the backseat all to herself.

The warmth from the heater didn't reach back there, and Shawna's toes were numb by the time they reached open farm country. Suddenly there was a terrible grinding noise followed by a loud clanging.

Shawna watched over Chuck's shoulder as the oil gauge took a nosedive. The temperature needle was in the hot zone. A red light came on, and then the engine died. Chuck steered to the side of the road, and the car coasted to a stop.

For a moment, no one said a word.

"What happened?" Shawna asked at last.

"I think we blew a rod," Chuck said glumly.

"Is that bad?"

"Oh, no. It's terrific if you don't mind starting from square one again!" Gene growled.

Beneath a cold, gray sky, they tramped silently to the nearest farmhouse. Chuck called a gas station to tow the car and give them a lift back to town. On the way, the fellow driving the tow truck told the boys that he restored old cars. He offered them four hundred dollars for the Mustang.

Shawna was wedged between the boys. "Take it and run!" she muttered.

Despite his bad mood, Gene agreed with her. Chuck was reluctant, and Shawna sensed he'd grown attached to the car. But after a whispered consultation with Gene, he, too, agreed to sell.

"So we wind up with a net profit of fifty bucks apiece," Gene grumbled a while later, as they sat in the Cayley's kitchen eating doughnuts and drinking hot cider to forget about their misery.

Remembering her promise to Courtney, Shawna decided to try one more time. "Those Christmas trees are still sitting in Courtney's driveway," she said casually.

Gene frowned. "You still pushing those trees, Squirt?"

But Shawna thought he looked as if he was beginning to weaken. She explained all of the paperwork she'd done the previous night. One chart itemized expenses, a graph showed how their profit would increase with each tree they sold, and she'd also drawn up a list of advertising ideas. She felt her hopes rising as she ran off to gather her facts.

"Maybe selling trees wouldn't be so bad," Shawna heard Gene say as she returned to the kitchen. "We could set up shop right here. That way, while we're at school, Mom could handle it."

Shawna joined them at the table. "Mom's too busy painting. Besides, we need a better location. You know, somewhere with a lot of traffic." She spread her charts out in front of the boys. "Look—this details our expenses. The figure includes a guesstimate as to what it might cost to rent that old gas station down on Main Street where the Boy Scouts used to always set up. Picking a tree is kind of traditional with people. They go back to the same place year after year."

"I say sell them here at the house and put what we save on rent in our pockets," Gene argued, and Chuck agreed.

Shawna was delighted that the boys were actually considering the project. She sat back as they pored over her charts and graphs, muttering to each other. She was quiet right up until the moment Gene said, "Split down the middle, it should be a good take."

"Now wait a second!" Shawna protested. "I want in!"

"No offense, Squirt, but you're a liability," her brother said.

"*Liability!*" she cried. "Wait a second. Don't forget, this was *my* idea!"

"Temper, temper," Gene teased. But he had a determined look in his eyes.

"I mean it, Gene. I want to be part of this," Shawna insisted.

Chuck spoke up. "It *was* her idea."

Shawna shot him a grateful glance.

"Okay, then let the Christmas tree queen do it—all of it, like she said before," Gene said with a shrug.

"You know as well as I do that I can't do it by myself!" Shawna cried. "I don't have any way of hauling the trees. And besides—"

"Exactly!" Gene shouted. "So leave it to us. You don't need the money as much as we do."

"I'll remember that when I'm making out my Christmas list," Shawna said, annoyed. "Your name'll be the first to go!" A look of hurt and angry tears filled her eyes. She sprang up from the table and made it to her room before she really began crying. How could Gene be so selfish? She flung herself down on the bed, pummeling her pillow in rage and frustration. The ring of her bedside phone interrupted her tantrum. It was Courtney and Shawna told her what had just happened.

"And you let Gene get away with it? That isn't like you. Go right back in there and stand up for yourself," Courtney said indignantly.

Courtney was right, Shawna decided. She'd struggled all her life to hold her own with Gene. Now was no time to wimp out. Shawna thanked her friend, and headed back to the kitchen.

"Half-Pint's got a good head on her shoulders. Just look at these charts. I'm telling you, Gene, she'd be a real help to us," Shawna overheard Chuck saying as she approached the kitchen. Shamelessly, she stood out in the hall, listening.

"But we'd earn more if we did it ourselves. That's the bottom line," Gene persisted.

"I know. But we could use a third person to help with sales. You're pretty busy after school right now—when you don't have a game, you've got practice. And I've got stuff to do, too. I can't be here all the time, either."

There was a long silence. "Just for the record, I still think we should do it alone. But I'll leave the decision up to you," Gene said finally. He scraped back his chair and opened the back door. "Guess we better get started cleaning up the mess in the garage."

"Be right there," said Chuck.

As he crossed to the sink to rinse out his

cup, Shawna slipped into the kitchen. "So what's your decision. Am I in?" she asked Chuck eagerly.

A slow grin crept across Chuck's face. "Eavesdropping, huh? Yeah, you're in. After all, it *was* your idea."

She squealed in delight. "Thanks, Chuck! I owe you one. Do you want to break the news to Gene, or shall I?"

"He'll take it better coming from me."

"Okay." Shawna nodded. "You tell him, and I'll whip up some humongous sandwiches. Feeding him is the best way I know of working myself back into my brother's good graces."

Chuck headed for the door mussing her hair as he passed. "You're a good kid, Half-Pint."

Chapter Five

Courtney breathed a huge sigh of relief when Shawna phoned to give her the news.

"You saved my life! Thanks, Shawna. How'd you talk the guys into it?"

Shawna filled her in, giving her all the details. Courtney giggled. "Chuck patted you on the head? What'd you say?"

Shawna, who was lying on her bed, rolled onto her back and twisted the phone cord around one finger. "What *could* I say? 'Excuse me, Chuck, but I'm *not* three years old'?"

"At least he stood up to Gene on your behalf. That's better than nothing," Courtney said brightly.

Shawna admitted that she guessed it was.

"Gene told me that Chuck's going to borrow a grain truck from his uncle and we'll pick up the trees tomorrow after school."

"But Gene has basketball practice, doesn't he?"

"Yes, and he refuses to miss it. He says he'll come help us as soon as practice is over."

"So it'll be just you and Chuck?" Courtney sounded pleased. "That has definite romantic possibilities."

"Yeah—the possibility of breaking my back, among other things," Shawna said. "I don't see what's so romantic about that."

Courtney laughed. "I see what you mean. Hey, would you like me to talk to Brandon? Maybe he and the rest of the guys will help with the trees after practice."

"You mean the whole *team*?" Shawna asked, startled.

"Sure. Bribe 'em with food. That always works."

Shawna decided it sounded like fun. "All right," she said. "Tell Brandon we'll feed everybody burgers, fries, and soda here when the job's done."

"Better check with your mom first," Courtney suggested.

"She won't mind, if you and I do all the cooking in the garage. Dad won't care if we use his contraptions as long as we clean up afterward."

Once she was off the phone, Shawna made herb tea for her mother and herself and brought it to the studio. She surveyed the colorful pattern emerging on her mother's loom. "It's shaping up nicely, Mom," she said.

Her mother accepted the compliment and the tea with a smile. "Thanks, honey."

As they sipped their hot drinks, Shawna told her mother about her plans. Mrs. Cayley was enthusiastic about everything, including feeding the basketball team. "What a great idea," she said. "Many hands make light work. But many *stomachs* mean a lot of food. Make sure you have enough."

Shawna curled up in a chair and started making a grocery list. She'd need tons of potatoes and gallons of vegetable oil for frying the curly potato strips she intended to make with her father's gadget, not to mention the umpteen pounds of hamburger and several cases of soda. . . .

When Chuck and Gene came in from cleaning the garage, Shawna sprang the tree-moving plan on them.

"Anything that saves us work sounds good to me," Chuck said.

But Gene frowned. "I'm not so sure. I mean, what'll the guys think?"

"They'll think we're in the Christmas tree business, of course," Shawna said. "What's the big deal? Afraid of ruining your big-shot image? If you feel that way, then tell them it's Chuck's business—Chuck's and mine. *We* don't care what they think, do we, Chuck?"

Chuck grinned. "I just hope they want to buy some trees."

Gene finally agreed, but Shawna could tell he was uneasy about it. As popular as her brother was, no one would ever guess how much he worried about what people thought of him. Being partners with Gene wasn't going to be easy.

The next afternoon, Courtney came home with Shawna right after school to begin preparations. Having decided to serve the meal buffet style, they covered the bench in Mr. Cayley's work area with a bright table-cloth. Colorful paper plates, napkins, and plastic utensils gave the room a festive look. Shawna made an arrangement of pine clippings and pine cones, attached a perky red bow, and set it in the center of the bench.

"That looks nice. Smells nice, too." Courtney leaned over the centerpiece. She inhaled the pungent scent of pine. "I'd put it on the dining room table if I were you. The guys'll be so busy loading their plates, no one will notice it out here."

Shawna grinned. "Enough looking and smelling! Time to work!"

For the next couple of hours, the girls did

just that. By five-thirty, the brownies they'd baked were cooling on the kitchen counter. They'd used Mr. Cayley's patty-making machine to prepare the ground beef for the grill, and the curled potato strips were soaking in cold salt water, ready to fry.

"I guess we've done all we can do for the moment," Shawna said.

"Whew! Look at my blouse—it's covered with chocolate. I'm a mess!" exclaimed Courtney.

"Feel free to shower and change into something of mine," Shawna suggested. "I'll use the upstairs bathroom. Then we'll start cooking."

Shawna showered quickly, then picked through her closet. Since they planned to do the cooking in the garage, the heavy Navajo weave sweater that fell almost to her knees would keep her warm. Dark brown leggings and a pair of fur-lined boots completed her outfit.

Shawna brushed her hair back from her face, securing it with a colorful woven band that went well with her sweater. She was applying a bit of makeup when Courtney burst into her room wearing a fuzzy pink sweater of Shawna's over her own cranberry-red miniskirt and matching tights.

"There are trees all over your yard, but there's no sign of the guys. They must have gone back for another load," she reported.

"We'd better fire up the grill," Shawna said, and added, "You look terrific!"

"So do you. Maybe Chuck prefers the Native American look." Courtney shot her a cheeky grin. "Come on, let's go cook!"

A little while later, Shawna heard the truck pull into the driveway. When Courtney snapped on the outdoor light, she saw half a dozen cars being parked along the street.

"Looks like the whole team came," Courtney reported.

"What about Chuck? Do you see him?" Shawna asked.

"He's in the truck." Courtney watched a moment longer, then returned to the smoking grill. "They're unloading the last of those trees. We'd better hurry!"

Shawna and Courtney had just filled the last napkin-lined basket with sizzling fries when the door at the front of the garage burst open.

About a dozen guys thronged in with a boisterous blend of deep voices and loud laughter. Shawna glanced at one ruddy face after another but she didn't see Chuck.

"Get this show on the road, Squirt," Gene called. "We're starving!"

"Where's Chuck?" Shawna asked, trying to keep the hot fries out of the reach of thieving fingers.

"He's taking the grain truck back to his uncle.

Brewster followed in his car to bring him back to town. It shouldn't take them long."

Shawna hid her disappointment. "We may as well eat, then. Everything's ready now."

Gene lifted the lid of the ice chest, and the guys helped themselves to sodas. Shawna, still batting away hands bent on snitching fries, carried the basket into the house and put it on the dining room table next to the hamburgers and rolls. The fellows quickly began filling their plates, and the food vanished in no time.

Shawna scurried out to the garage to fix more burgers and fries, and Courtney followed. It wasn't long before the guys began drifting out to join them.

"Move over, Courtney, and hand me that turner. I'm an expert at this," bragged George Heck.

"Make mine medium well," called Jimmy Jones.

George grinned and shot back, "This isn't Burger King. I make 'em *my* way."

As Shawna began preparing the potatoes, Kenny Kane came over to her and watched her use her father's curly-fry invention.

"That doesn't look too hard. Let me have a try," he said after a moment.

Kenny was tall and slender, with straw-colored hair. The color of his eyes was hard to distinguish behind his heavy-rimmed glasses, and his friendly smile revealed a row of wire braces. Responding with a smile of her own, Shawna stepped aside. "Be my guest."

Courtney gave Kenny a grin. "Take the kitchen into the garage, and you guys all become instant chefs!"

Kenny had just taken the crisp, golden fries out of the vat when Shawna heard the walk-through door open. She felt her heart begin to pound madly. "I thought the deal was that if the guys moved the trees, the girls would cook. What's going on here?" Chuck called out, smiling.

"Wait a second! We *did* cook," Shawna protested.

"Of course we did. Pay no attention to him," Courtney chimed in.

"They just took over," Shawna added.

"What good luck," said Chuck. "Since you're free, how about getting me a plate? I'm running on empty. While you're at it, get *three* plates. Brewster's coming, too, and he's got a friend with him."

"A friend?" Shawna echoed. "Who?"

"Me," trilled a feminine voice.

Shawna and Courtney turned toward the door, as did every male in the room. Melissa Doty waltzed in on the arm of John Brewster, looking like a rosy cloud in her pink earmuffs, fuzzzy pink coat, and trendy pink leg warmers.

48

"I hope you don't mind my crashing like this," Melissa chirped. "Brewster and I have a study date. He said it'd be okay if we grabbed a quick bite first." Her voice was sweet, and as her dimples flashed, her smile dazzled.

Brewster looked proud to have Melissa at his side. "It *is* okay, isn't it?" he asked.

"No problem. The more the merrier," Gene said cheerfully.

Melissa batted her eyelashes and replied, "Thanks, Gene. You're so sweet!"

"I'll get those plates," Shawna muttered.

Chuck pulled his gaze away from Melissa long enough to smile at her. "Thanks, Shawna."

Shawna's rebellious heart tipped. He'd actually called her by her real name! If only he'd look at her the way every guy in the room was looking at Melissa!

For the next hour or so, Shawna's guests meandered back and forth between the garage and the dining room. Melissa complimented the food and admired the artwork on the walls. Pausing to admire the centerpiece, she suggested, "You might mix in some cinnamon sticks and dried apple slices to give the arrangement additional color and texture." She giggled and added, "Oh no, I'm starting to sound like my mother! I've been helping her in her craft shop." Though she was talking to Shawna, every guy within earshot was concentrating on every word that came out of her mouth.

"She's so full of herself," Shawna grumbled to Courtney much later in the evening when everyone else had gone home.

Courtney looked up from scouring the grease vat. "I don't have a problem with her, as long as she doesn't get any ideas about 'studying' with Brandon."

In her mind's eye, Shawna kept seeing the way Chuck and the rest of the guys had reacted to Melissa. Was Chuck still thinking of asking her to the dance, or would Brewster be taking her? Was Chuck as jealous of Brewster as Shawna was of Melissa? Shawna sighed and wrinkled her nose.

"I've never been jealous before," she admitted. "I don't like the way it feels."

"Then don't be."

"If only it was that easy!" Shawna dried her hands on a dish towel, then hung it over a chair to dry.

"That's because you're only focusing on how pretty Melissa is. There are some things about her that aren't so attractive," Courtney said. "Once you discover them, you'll be so thankful you're not like that, you'll never be jealous of her again."

Shawna thought it over for a minute, then laughed. "Court, that's so ridiculous, it almost makes sense!"

Courtney laughed, too. "Anyway, you had fun, didn't you, in spite of Melissa?"

"Yes," Shawna admitted, "I did. Did I tell you Chuck actually called me 'Shawna'? Not 'Half-Pint' but 'Shawna'?"

Courtney grinned. "Only about sixteen times."

Chapter Six

After school the next day, Shawna waved good-bye to Courtney, who had cheerleading practice, then headed for the exit at the north end of the school building. As she rounded the last turn in senior hall, she saw Chuck at his locker.

Shawna's heart flip-flopped as she got closer to him. To slacken her pace would be too obvious. "Hi, Chuck," she said casually as she passed by.

"Half-Pint! Wait up and I'll give you a lift home," he called after her.

Naturally, Shawna waited.

"I got some scrap lumber from Mr. Fallon in shop," Chuck told her, falling into step beside her. "It's enough to make a couple of signs. I loaded it onto the truck during my free hour."

He held the door open, and Shawna ducked under his extended arm. A blast of frigid wind discouraged further conversation as they walked to his truck.

Once they were seated inside, Chuck jerked a thumb toward the bed of the truck where odd-shaped pieces of wood were piled.

"It's only plywood, but it won't look too bad once we've given it a coat of paint."

"We've got some white paint in the garage," Shawna said. "Brushes, too."

"Good! Then we can get started right away. Unless you have something else to do," he added.

"No, nothing. Maybe we could make some posters, too, and tack them up around town."

"Fine," Chuck agreed. "I should warn you, though, I'm not too good at lettering posters."

"I bet Mom'll help us. She's terrific at stuff like that," said Shawna.

The Cayleys' garage soon rang with the sound of Chuck's sawing and hammering. Admiring his sure-handed way with tools, Shawna pried the lid off a half-empty can of white paint, found a stick, and began to stir it.

"I was thinking—we could make up some bookmarks on Dad's computer and print the address on them and the price of the trees," Shawna said eagerly as they worked.

"And leave them at the public library? That's a good idea."

Shawna thought it over a moment longer. "What if we printed a coupon on the back of the bookmarks? We could offer a dollar off to anyone who buys a tree from us. We could pass them out at school, too."

"Except that it's adults, not kids, who buy Christmas trees," Chuck pointed out.

There was nothing critical in his voice. He was simply giving her feedback. Encouraged, Shawna used him for a sounding board on several other promotional ideas. The one Chuck liked best was donating a tree to the local radio station. Each year, WXBN put up a tree in the lobby of their building, and encouraged their listening audience to stop by and hang mittens and caps on the tree. The donated items were then given to underprivileged children.

"Maybe they'd give us a free plug on the air," Chuck said.

Shawna nodded. "And even if they don't, it'll be a tree well spent."

Chuck hammered a few more nails into the big freestanding sign he'd built. "If you want to start painting this one, I'll start working on another. We'll put them both in the yard, one facing east, the other west. That way, we'll attract people going in both directions."

"You're pretty good at this. It looks great," Shawna said.

Chuck grinned. "Thanks. Grab one end and we'll move it so you can get started painting."

Chuck helped her move the sign onto the drop cloth she'd spread on the floor. While Shawna concentrated on her painting, Chuck began building the second sign.

A few minutes later, Shawna's mother came into the garage.

"I thought I heard hammering," she said. "What on earth are you two doing?"

Shawna explained their promotional plans, and it didn't take much coaxing to enlist her mother's help. Shawna found some poster board, and soon Mrs. Cayley was busily lettering poster after poster.

It was almost six o'clock and pitch dark outside by the time Gene came home from basketball practice. He was tired and hungry, so they decided to order in fried chicken.

As the four of them sat around the kitchen table, Shawna listened while Chuck told Gene how much they'd accomplished in the past few hours.

"Don't you think we should give our business a name?" Shawna asked.

They brainstormed for a while, trying to come up with something catchy. Finally Mrs. Cayley said, "How about 'Season's Greetings'?"

"Hey, I like it!" Gene exclaimed. "What do you think, Chuck?"

"Sounds good. Shawna?"

"Fine by me," Shawna said, glad that her mother had suggested a name they could all agree on. Carrying the plates to the sink, she added, "Now that's settled, we'd better get back to work."

Gene yawned broadly. "Sorry. You're going to have to get along without me. I'm dead on my feet, and I've still got homework."

"Why don't you call it quits for tonight?" Mrs. Cayley suggested. "You can finish up tomorrow after school."

After Chuck had gone home, Shawna sat down at her father's computer. It didn't take long to create coupon bookmarks, but cutting them apart was tedious.

It was almost midnight when Shawna snapped out the light and tumbled into bed. She closed her eyes, and her thoughts immediately shifted from business to romance. How much did Chuck really care for Melissa? Was it just a passing attraction, or was he in love with her? Would he decide not to ask her to the dance, since she seemed to be making a major play for Brewster? And if he didn't ask Melissa, was there the tiniest chance that he might ask Shawna?

Shawna drifted off to sleep at last, with no answers to any of her questions.

*   *   *

The next morning, Shawna overslept. Gene left for school before she had a chance to show him the bookmarks, so she slipped them into her backpack. On her way home from school, she'd stop by the library and drop them off.

Shawna raced into the building just as the five-minute bell rang through the corridors of Woodrow Wilson High.

" 'Morning, Half-Pint," a familiar voice said behind her.

"Oh, hi, Chuck! Wait a second—I've got something for you." Shawna rummaged in her backpack and pulled out the bookmarks. In her haste, she broke the rubber band, scattering bookmarks all over the hallway.

Chuck helped her pick them up. "What *is* all this stuff?" he asked.

"Bookmarks, remember? I mentioned them last night."

He laughed. "Boy, you're a fast worker!"

"Chuck? Hurry up—we're going to be late for class," a sugary voice called.

Shawna whirled around to see Melissa Doty standing a few yards away, tall, elegant, and shapely in snug-fitting designer jeans and a pink silk shirt. The dimpled smile she gave Chuck made Shawna's heart sink.

"Go on. I'll get the rest of them," Shawna mumbled, suddenly feeling short, frumpy, and shapeless.

Chuck started to give her the bookmarks he'd gathered, but Shawna shook her head. "Pass them out to kids in your classes."

"Better hurry. Final bell's about to ring," he warned, going over to join Melissa.

As the two of them were swallowed up by the crowd in the hall, Shawna's pride in the bookmarks she'd created evaporated into thin air. She felt like dropping them in the nearest trash can.

But she didn't. Throughout the day, Shawna passed out the bookmarks to classmates, friends, and teachers. By the time the final bell rang, she still had several dozen left.

Courtney had to cheer at a basketball game at four-thirty. But she needed to pick up her cheerleading outfit from the dry cleaner first, so she offered to drop Shawna off at the library. The head librarian agreed to put the bookmarks in the rack where patrons could help themselves.

Shawna walked home and went straight to the garage where she began brushing a clear weatherproof coating on the posters her mother had made the previous evening. She hadn't been working long when Mrs. Cayley came out to letter the signs Chuck had built.

"I wonder what's happened to Chuck," Shawna said. "I was sure he'd be here to help."

"Something probably came up." Her mother dipped her brush in green paint and began bordering the first sign in holly.

At four-thirty the phone rang. Shawna dashed for the house, hoping it would be Chuck. It was. "I thought I'd stay for the game," he said. "Why don't you come watch? We'll finish the signs together tomorrow."

"I don't think so," Shawna murmured.

"Okay, then. See you later."

After they hung up, Shawna frowned, wondering if he had been planning on staying for the game all along, or if someone had talked him into it. Melissa Doty maybe? Shawna's spirits sank. As she drove around town in her mother's car, putting up the posters, she kept seeing images of Chuck and Melissa sitting close together on the bleachers in the gym, cheering the Rockets on to victory.

By the time she returned home, Mrs. Cayley had finished lettering the freestanding signs. *They are so professional looking*, Shawna thought, with their bright borders of holly and red berries. She gave the garage a good cleaning, then went into the kitchen. Her mother was cooking something that smelled delicious.

"The signs look great, Mom," Shawna said. "Thanks for all your help."

Her mother smiled. "Anything to keep my kids happy. After you wash up, why don't you set the table, honey? Gene ought to be home any minute now."

Gene came in the front door a moment later, hollering, "Where's Shawna?" He stormed into the kitchen, and Shawna could tell by the look on his face the game had not gone well.

"Who won?" Mrs. Cayley asked.

"Tremont. But what can you expect when the referee is blind as a bat? He called a foul on me in the last two seconds of the game, and I never even touched the guy! Tremont won by one point! But never mind that." Gene turned to Shawna and waved a wrinkled bookmark under her nose. "Just what's the idea of passing these things out all over school?"

Shawna shrugged. "It's advertising. How can we sell any trees if nobody knows about it?"

"That's the dumbest thing I ever heard!" Gene yelled. "Like all the kids at school are going to rush right over here and buy a tree!"

"Maybe they won't, but their parents might," Shawna told him. "With the dollar-off coupon, we'll have the cheapest trees in town."

"Why don't you grow up? Would you talk to her, Mom?" Gene pleaded.

Mrs. Cayley took the bookmark and looked it over. "Calm down, Gene. It's a perfectly acceptable form of advertising. I know you're upset about losing the game, but don't take it out on Shawna."

"Forget the game! Having a dork for a sister is what's *really* upsetting me—a dork who hasn't got brains enough to know what's cool and what isn't!" he thundered.

"I showed them to Chuck. *He* didn't think they were dorky. He passed them out, too," Shawna said angrily.

"No, he didn't," Gene retorted. "He thought it was a dumb idea, only he wouldn't say so. Here are the ones you gave him." Gene took out a stack of bookmarks from his coat pocket and flung them down on the table.

Shawna stared at them, appalled. Had she embarrassed Chuck, too? Was that the reason he'd stayed for the game instead of coming over to help? She swallowed hard around the sudden lump in her throat.

"I think it would be a good idea if you cooled down a little before you talk about this anymore," their mother said to Gene. "You *are* partners, after all."

"Not anymore," Gene growled. "Maybe Chuck can put up with her, but I can't. Either she quits or I quit!"

"That's ridiculous," Mrs. Cayley snapped. "Sit down. After dinner, I want the three of you to get together and work this out."

"What's there to work out?" Shawna said, fighting back tears. "Gene didn't have time to help us last night or tonight, and now it looks like Chuck's too busy, too. At this rate, I'll end up doing all the work anyway. The two of them can run the business right into the ground. *I* quit!"

Shawna stormed out of the kitchen, too angry to even cry. In her room, she flipped open her geometry book. She shut everything else out and concentrated on her homework. A while later, her mother knocked at the door.

"Shawna? Chuck's downstairs. He'd like to talk to you a minute."

"I don't want to talk to *him*. Make up an excuse for me, okay, Mom?"

There was a long pause. Then her mother said in a low voice, "Shawna, you really should give him a chance to explain."

Shawna's pride had already been shot down. Even now, Gene's words were ringing in her ears: *He thought it was a dumb idea, only he wouldn't say so.* She couldn't face Chuck, she just couldn't!

"Honey? Are you coming?" her mother asked softly.

Shawna didn't reply. She held her breath a moment, then listened to her mother's receding footsteps. The print on the page suddenly blurred before her eyes. She closed her book and snapped out the light. In the darkness the tears she'd been holding back for so long finally came.

Chapter Seven

Keeping out of Chuck's way at school was easy for Shawna—she'd memorized his schedule weeks ago. But avoiding her own house, now the business location for Season's Greetings, was another story.

"How long do you think you can keep this up?" asked Courtney, as they left school together late one afternoon.

"It isn't so bad," Shawna said. "I finished my homework while I waited for you. Anyway, what am I supposed to do? I can't go home with Chuck there."

"It's *your* house, not his."

"I know. But all I care about is staying away from him."

"Why? Are you angry with him? Do you hate him?"

"No, of course not!" Shawna cried.

Putting on her coat, Courtney rolled her eyes in exasperation. "You don't hate him. You aren't angry. In that case, I fail to see the point of your dodging out of sight every time he comes within a hundred feet of you."

"Those bookmarks! I embarrassed him. Gene said so. He's really mad at me, and now I'm embarrassed myself."

"Gene's still in a vile mood over losing that last game. He's taking it out on you, and you're letting him get away with it!" Courtney said.

"If you'd rather I didn't go home with you anymore, I can find someplace else to hang out," Shawna said stiffly.

"Don't be silly!" Courtney exclaimed. "You're always welcome at my house, you know that. It's just that I don't understand why you don't straighten things out with Gene and Chuck."

"I don't know how," Shawna confessed as they walked out of the building toward Courtney's car.

"I don't see what's so difficult," Courtney said. "You told me the guys aren't selling many trees on their own. Obviously they need your help."

That was true. The trees weren't moving at all. But it didn't change Shawna's dread of facing Chuck. In trying to impress him with

64

how grown-up she was, she had accomplished just the opposite. It made her blush to think how childish those bookmarks must have seemed to him.

Shawna had dinner at Courtney's house. She helped with the dishes afterward, and dialed her home number.

To her dismay, Chuck answered the phone. Stammering a little, she asked to speak to her mother.

"Sorry, she's not here."

"How about Gene, then?"

"Just a second . . . Gene? It's Half-Pint," Shawna heard Chuck call. A moment later, Gene's voice came over the line, sounding annoyed.

"Make it quick, Squirt."

"I'm at Courtney's. I need a ride home."

"Right now? Dad's home and we're watching the video of my last game."

"Dad's home? Great! Tell him I need a ride." Without giving her brother a chance to object, Shawna hung up the phone, then waited by the window.

When a pair of headlights beamed up the driveway, Shawna put her coat on. "Thanks for being such a good friend, Court. See you tomorrow. Thanks for dinner, Mrs. Scott," she said.

But when she stepped outside, Shawna saw that instead of her father's car, Chuck's truck was waiting in the driveway. The door on the driver's side opened, and Chuck stepped out.

"Gene said you needed a ride," he said.

"I told him to send Dad," Shawna mumbled, flustered.

"Don't get mad at your brother. I offered." Chuck circled the truck and opened the passenger's door so she could get in. But instead of closing the door, he stood there looking at her. "How come you've been avoiding me?" he asked after a silent moment.

"What makes you think I've been doing that?" Shawna asked in return.

"Number one, you haven't been around to sell trees. Number two, you haven't been home at all. And number three, I haven't run into you at school," he said. "In fact, this is the first time I've seen you all week."

Shawna's stomach began to turn. "I'm not going to help with the trees," she told him.

"That's all? No explanation?" Chuck said, after another long moment.

Shawna kept quiet.

At last he went back around the front of the truck and climbed inside.

It was a silent ride home. Shawna had her hand on the door handle, prepared to dash into the house the second he stopped the truck. But he drove right past her house.

"Hey!" she protested.

Chuck glanced over at her. "Are you going to tell me why you're angry? Or am I going to have to circle the block a couple more times?"

"Come on, Chuck. I haven't seen Dad in a week and a half. Anyway, I'm not angry. Now please, back up and let me out."

"I thought we were friends, Shawna."

"We are."

"Then why can't you just tell me what's been bugging you? This Christmas tree deal was all your idea. One day you're full of plans. The next, you quit and then make yourself scarce. All I want is an explanation."

"It was the bookmarks. Gene thought it was a stupid, childish idea," she mumbled finally.

Chuck looked genuinely surprised. "The bookmarks? You quit over the *bookmarks*?"

"Gene didn't like any of my ideas. He said either *I* quit or *he* would." She hesitated a moment, then added in a rush, "He told me you thought the bookmarks were a lame idea, too. I'm sorry if I embarrassed you."

"Did I say I was embarrassed?"

"No. But obviously you were, or you would have passed them out instead of giving them all to Gene."

"I didn't give them to Gene. He took them," Chuck retorted.

Shawna frowned. "But he led me to be-lieve . . . then you *didn't* think it was a stu-pid idea? You weren't embarrassed?"

Chuck grinned. "Of course not."

"Then why did Gene act like you were?"

"I don't know. Maybe because *he* was em-barrassed." Having circled the block another time, Chuck pulled up to the curb in front of Shawna's house. Letting the motor run, he turned in the seat to face her. "You know how Gene is. He's got this image thing."

Shawna nodded. "Yeah. I guess I should have talked it over with him before I made the bookmarks since he was a partner, too."

"Probably," Chuck agreed. "Seems like the problem has been poor communication. What do you say we try it again?"

"You mean, be partners again? All three of us?" Shawna asked. "What about Gene?"

"He may not admit it, but he's beginning to realize that we need you," Chuck said. "After all, you're the one with all the ideas and the enthusiasm. You've also got more time than he does. Face it, Gene's a lot bet-ter at basketball than he is at business. So what do you say? Want to give it another shot?"

Suddenly Shawna felt as if a huge boulder had been lifted off her heart. "You bet I will! And Chuck? Thanks for . . . well, you know, understanding."

"Hey, that's what friends are for." Chuck

punched her shoulder lightly. "See you tomorrow, kid."

"Why don't you come in?" Shawna suggested, not even bothered by his calling her "kid." "If Season's Greetings is going to be a success, we've got a lot more planning to do."

"Well, I don't know. Your father's just come home . . . maybe we should wait until tomorrow," he added, not wanting to intrude.

"Dad won't care," Shawna assured him. "And I bet he can give us some good advice on the project."

The minute they walked in the door, Shawna's father greeted her with a wide grin and a big hug. "There's my girl!"

"Daddy!" Laughing, she returned the hug. "How was your trip?"

"Long, tiring, and I missed my family something terrible," he said.

"What about your electronic piecrust maker? Anybody interested?" Shawna asked as she took off her jacket.

"A little."

The sparkle in her father's blue eyes told Shawna he was being far too modest. With a little encouragement, he told her that the research and development department at a major manufacturer was very impressed with his invention and had promised to contact him right after Christmas.

"Daddy, that's great news!" Anxious not to

leave Chuck out, Shawna explained that the machine her father had invented not only mixed pie dough, but rolled it out as well.

Shawna, Chuck, and Gene began to talk about the Christmas tree project with Mr. Cayley. Gene had already explained why there was a forest of trees in the driveway, and as Shawna had predicted, her father was interested in their venture and offered some great suggestions. Gene didn't challenge Shawna's right to rejoin the partnership. Maybe Chuck was right—perhaps Gene had realized that they needed her. Whatever the reason, he was willing to listen when she again suggested that their location was all wrong.

Her mother, who had arrived home from an art exhibition in time to catch the end of their conversation, agreed. "You really need a spot near other businesses."

"Absolutely," Mr. Cayley added.

"Shawna's probably right. Maybe we should see about renting that old gas station on Main Street," Chuck said.

"I guess it wouldn't hurt to call and ask how much it would cost," Gene conceded. "I wonder who it belongs to?"

Chuck snapped his fingers. "Hey! What about Melissa Doty? Her mother's craft shop is right next door to the station. They probably know who owns the property."

"Good idea. Shawna, why don't you give her a call?" said Mr. Cayley.

Suddenly Shawna's good mood evaporated. All it took was the mention of Melissa's name. Reluctantly, Shawna paged through the phone book and dialed the number, thinking that if they *did* rent the old gas station, Melissa would be their closest neighbor.

"Something wrong, Half-Pint?" Chuck asked.

"The line's busy." She hung up the phone, avoiding his gaze.

"No problem. I'll stop by her house on my way home," he offered. He immediately stood up and reached for his jacket.

Shawna echoed the rest of her family as they said good night to Chuck. But it hurt to see how eager he was to visit Melissa.

The next morning, Chuck caught up with Shawna at her locker.

"Melissa's mother not only knew the owner, but she had his phone number," he told her. "When I called him, he said we were welcome to use the property as long as we cleaned up after ourselves. We can even use the building to get out of the cold."

"How much?"

Chuck's grin broadened. "No charge. He said he liked to encourage kids to set themselves up in business—it's good for the economy."

"Really? That's great!" Shawna beamed. "Let's give him a tree. It's the least we can do."

Chuck agreed. As the bell rang, he said, "We've got the four-day Thanksgiving weekend coming up. That should give us time to move the trees and get everything ready. Then we can sit back and wait for the money to start rolling in."

Shawna's pleasure in his good news was cut short all too soon.

"So there you are!" Melissa Doty rested a slender hand on Chuck's arm. "I've been looking all over for you, Chuck. I'm just dying to know what Mr. Smith had to say. Did you get in touch with him?"

At his nod and smile, Melissa cried, "Oh, that's terrific! You guys'll be right next door! Shawna, you better go easy on the guys. You know what they say about all work and no play. We certainly don't want Chuck turning dull!"

Shawna tried to smile, but it was a major effort. She wasn't sure how much of Melissa's "good neighbor policy" she could take over the next few weeks.

Chapter Eight

Thanksgiving day was a departure from the Cayleys' traditional noonday meal. Shawna, Gene, their parents, and Chuck began moving the trees early in the morning.

The pumps at the old gas station had been removed years ago. As the day progressed, Christmas trees turned the entire area surrounding the garage and office into a giant green forest.

After Mr. and Mrs. Cayley went home, Shawna strung the plate glass window of the office with outdoor lights. The electricity hadn't been turned on yet, but a phone call to the utility company would soon take care of that. The boys continued unwrapping trees and trimming away unwanted branches.

Shawna had devised a color-coded system for marking and pricing the trees according to height. Chuck marked off a pole in feet and as Gene measured each tree against it, Shawna tied on the appropriate colored tag. Then the boys built some stands to prop up the best-shaped trees.

As the afternoon sun drifted westward, all three of them took a break, sitting on the floor of the office. "It'd be nice if we could light up the whole lot," Shawna said. "I know it's extra work, but look around. We don't want to be shoddy by comparison," she said and gestured with a mittened hand.

Through the window they could see the faded brick structure that housed Doty's Dabblings. Melissa Doty's mother had decorated her shop with evergreen boughs and velvet ribbons. On one side stood a hotel all decked out in holiday trimming. Across the street an elegant stone church displayed an elaborate nativity scene on the lawn, and diagonally across the intersection stood the Red Caboose, a quaint coffee shop fashioned from an old railway car. Decorative lanterns hung from every beribboned and garland-wrapped iron post lining the walkway.

"What time shall we open shop tomorrow?" Shawna asked.

"Don't count on me until after lunch," said Gene.

"*After lunch!* You lazy thing!" Shawna cried.

"I've got practice in the morning. And watch who you call lazy." Gene gave her a playful punch on the shoulder, and flashed her a wide smile. With Chuck looking on, Shawna resisted the impulse to punch him back, smiling instead.

"I'm hungry. Let's lock up and go home," Chuck said as the courthouse tower clock tolled four times.

"Just a minute," said Shawna. "That red bow on the door looks kind of bare."

"Hurry up, Shawna, the temperature's dropping," Gene complained.

"Be right there." Hastily, Shawna added a small silver bell and an evergreen bough to the bow.

"I know one sure way of getting her out of here!" Gene turned around and made a dramatic dive for Shawna's feet. Before she could protest, Chuck grabbed her under her arms. Both boys trotted to the grain truck Chuck had borrowed again and dumped her in the back. Laughing at her pretended outrage, Chuck ran back to padlock the office. Then he and Gene hopped into the cab of the truck.

Laughing, too, Shawna pounded on the sides of the grain truck, yelling, "That's all right. I'll ride back here. I'm tough. I can take it! I am woman, hear me roar!"

The motor rumbled, drowning out her voice. As the truck moved forward through the lot, the cold breeze stung Shawna's eyes. "Hey, you guys! It's freezing back here!"

Chuck's door flew open. "That sounded more like a whimper than a roar to me," he teased. "Come on, Half-Pint. We're so big-hearted that we're going to let you ride up front with the big boys."

They all joked on the way home, and it was apparent everyone was in the holiday spirit. "The day after Thanksgiving should be a busy one. I'll open up about eight in the morning. How about it, Half-Pint? Can you be ready that early?" Chuck asked as he pulled into the driveway.

"No problem," Shawna said as she and Gene got out. She waved as the truck pulled away.

Gene headed toward the house, his nose in the air. "Something smells fantastic. Thanksgiving dinner at last!"

The next morning, Shawna put on her long johns and dressed in her warmest jeans and three layers of color-coordinated sweatshirts. She searched the attic for more lights and decorations, and hauled out a kerosene heater and her transistor radio.

Chuck pulled into the driveway a few minutes before eight. Shawna met him on the front step. "Morning," she said, smiling.

Chuck indicated the odds and ends at her feet. "Is this it—I hope?"

Shawna nodded and helped him carry everything out to the truck.

On the ride downtown, Chuck offered to phone the utility company at nine. Shawna's heart sank as he went next door to use the phone.

Was Melissa there? Was he using the phone call as an excuse to see her? *As if he needs an excuse!* Shawna thought. Knowing Melissa, she'd fall all over him with or without an excuse!

When Chuck came back, Shawna couldn't bring herself to ask if Melissa had been in the shop. "Are they going to turn on the power right away?" she asked.

He warmed his hands over the kerosene heater in the office. "There's a pretty stiff service charge," he told her.

The amount he named made Shawna gasp. "That *is* a lot! We only need it for three or four weeks."

"Still, I don't see how we can get along without electricity, do you?" Chuck asked.

Shawna sighed. "Maybe we better wait and talk it over with Gene."

By midmorning, two teachers had bought trees, bringing bookmark coupons. But otherwise sales were pitifully slow. Lunchtime came and went with no sign of Gene. Shawna and Chuck agreed to alternate taking breaks so they wouldn't miss any customers.

"Did you or Gene ever contact WXBN about donating the mitten tree?" Shawna asked when Chuck came back from lunch.

"We didn't quite know how to go about it." Chuck sat down on an empty crate. He propped his back against the office wall and watched as Shawna stenciled *Season's Greetings* across the plate glass window.

"You call the audience participation line," Shawna said.

"And talk on the air?" Chuck looked doubtful.

"Sure, why not? It'll be good for business."

"I guess," he said, without much enthusiasm.

"I'll do it if you want," Shawna offered.

Chuck grinned at her. "Good idea. You're gutsy, Half-Pint. I've always liked that about you."

His praise made her feel warm all over. "I hope Gene's not listening in," Shawna admitted. "If I make a fool of myself, he'll probably kick me out of the family."

Chuck laughed. "Don't worry. If he does, I'll adopt you."

Terrific, Shawna thought. *Will he ever realize I'm not a little kid?*

Just then the bells Shawna had hung from

the door tinkled. Melissa Doty hurried in and closed the door behind her, pretty as a picture in her fuzzy pink coat. She flashed a sparkling smile at them both. "Hi, Chuck! Hi, Shawna. How's business?"

Chuck leapt to his feet, beaming at her. "If you're looking for the best tree in town, you came to the right place!"

"My, aren't you the eager salesman! I just *adore* eagerness in a guy." Melissa fluttered her thick bronze-colored lashes, and Shawna noticed Chuck didn't ask *her* if she had something in her eye.

Disgusted with her flirting, Shawna excused herself, saying, "I'll go make that phone call now."

"You have to make a call? Use the phone in the shop. No, really! I insist," Melissa said when Shawna tried to decline.

"Thanks." Shawna forced a politeness she was far from feeling.

Next door, Mrs. Doty welcomed her warmly. When Shawna asked permission to use the phone, she said, "It's in the back room, dear. Help yourself." *How could such a nice woman have such a phony daughter?* Shawna wondered.

She looked up the station number, organized her thoughts, then dialed the number.

"WXBN. You're on the air," came the mellow voice of the afternoon talk-show host.

Suddenly Shawna felt all of her muscles

tighten. "This is Shawna Cayley at Season's Greetings downtown. I'm calling to see if you have a mitten tree yet," she said, trying her best to keep a level tone.

"If you have mittens to donate, just bring them to the station. Does that answer your question?"

"No, not exactly. What I mean to say is, I want to donate the *tree*. My brother and his friend and I have a lot of trees. We're downtown at the old gas station on Main Street."

"You're giving away trees? Hey, wonderful! If you'd like to leave your number, I'm sure there are a lot of listeners out there who could use a free tree."

"No! We're not giving them away, we're *selling* them," Shawna said quickly.

"I'm sorry. We don't take advertising on this program."

"I know," Shawna said, breaking out in a nervous sweat. "I wasn't trying to sell *you* a tree! I wanted to *give* you one. For the mitten tree."

The talk-show host laughed. "Oh, I see. Well, thanks a lot, but I'm afraid that's already been taken care of. The station manager picked one up this morning."

"Oh. Well—uh—good-bye." Shawna hung up the phone and buried her burning face in her hands. *What a bummer!* she thought. *I sounded like a total idiot!* Suddenly Melissa pranced in with Chuck right behind her. She was giggling so much, she could hardly speak. "I'm sorry. I shouldn't laugh, but honestly, Shawna, that was hysterical! Talk about confused! You really had that poor guy going."

Shawna's face flamed. "I made a complete fool of myself!"

"Oh, not a *complete* fool," Melissa said. "And even if you did, what does it matter? Hardly anyone we know actually *listens* to that hokey station."

"I hope Gene wasn't listening! He will *definitely* disown me!" Shawna moaned.

Chuck touched her shoulder. "You tried. It wasn't your fault the guy was slow on the uptake. And as for Gene disowning you, my adoption offer still stands."

"Oh, thanks a lot! That's encouraging!" Shawna bolted out of the room, through the shop, and back to Season's Greetings.

Chuck was alone when he returned. "Have you got any use for the clippings from the trees?" he asked after an uncomfortable silence.

"The pine boughs? I don't think so. Why?" Shawna asked.

"Melissa says they'd make nice wreaths. She'd like to have them if you don't need them."

Still upset over Melissa's reaction to the radio call, Shawna said sharply, "Today the clippings, tomorrow . . ."

Chuck cut her off, a puzzled look on his face. "What's the matter, Shawna?"

Shawna jutted out a stubborn chin. "I could make wreaths, and *we* could sell them. After all, they're *our* trees. Why should she profit from them?"

She knew she sounded small and petty, but Melissa's mocking giggle still rang in her ears. Not to mention the outrageous way she kept throwing herself at Chuck! "If you want to give them to her, then go ahead," she said crossly.

Shawna marched out the door just as Gene came across the street. Worried that he might have heard the broadcast, she braced herself for his chastising. But as he drew closer, she saw that he didn't look mad. His expression was faintly apologetic.

"I ate lunch at Heck's house after practice, and I kind of lost track of the time. But the good news is Heck and some of the other guys are going to stop by later. That should more than make up for time lost." Gene glanced around. "Where's Chuck?"

So he *hadn't* been listening to the radio. Relieved, Shawna jerked a thumb toward the office. "You two can mind the store for a while. I'm going to take a little walk."

Chapter Nine

Shawna tried to walk off her frustration, circling the downtown square. She paused to look in the window of Mahogany's, her favorite dress shop. One mannequin had on a beautiful strapless dress. The deep purple velvet made Shawna think of a dusky sky. She closed her eyes and pictured herself wearing it to the holiday dance with Chuck. Her hair was a red-gold cloud about her bare shoulders, and her feet were as light as air. . . .

Swept along by the pleasant fantasy, Shawna went into the store and searched the racks until she found the purple dress in her size. In the dressing room, she shed her sweatshirts, jeans, long johns, and socks. The plush satin-lined velvet glided over her body. *Is it just the dimness of the light,* Shawna wondered, *or does the gown really bring out a violet hue in my eyes?*

Bare-legged, her pink toenails peeping up at her, she walked out to the full-length mirror in the main showroom. The snug-fitting bodice narrowed to a V just below her waist. The skirt of the dress was gently gathered, and folds of velvet cascaded past her hips, ending a little below her knees. The look was simple, yet elegantly sophisticated.

Shawna gathered up her windblown hair in one hand. Lifting it off her shoulders, she turned to one side in an attempt to see the back of the dress.

"Shawna?"

The sound of Chuck's voice took Shawna by surprise, and she whirled around. He pulled off his knitted cap and stepped closer to her.

"I thought I saw you come in here." His wide-eyed gaze swept over her. "What are you doing in that dress?"

Face flushing, Shawna turned back toward the mirror, meeting his eyes in the glass. "I took a break to do a little shopping."

"Nice choice." The startled expression seemed frozen on his face. "Is it for the dance?" he asked.

Not knowing how to answer, Shawna ignored the question. "I guess you're thinking I should get back to work."

"No, not really. I just wanted to tell you . . ." Chuck's eyes swept over her once again, from her tousled hair to her pink-tipped toes. His color deepened. "I didn't realize you were shopping." He hesitated before he completed his thought. "I shouldn't have bothered you."

"That's okay. What did you want to tell me?" Shawna asked.

"Never mind. It'll keep until you get back." Chuck beat a hasty retreat, slamming the door behind him.

Shawna had twenty dollars in her pocket, and she used it as a deposit to put the dress on layaway. But as she walked back to Season's Greetings, she couldn't believe she'd done it. She didn't even have a date for the dance! What crazy impulse had driven her to buy the dress?

While Shawna was gone, Gene's basketball buddies had dropped by. George had cut the end off a frayed extension cord and was installing a new plug. Courtney's boyfriend, Brandon, was helping Gene and Chuck string lights around the lot. Kenny and Jimmy were on the roof of the building, putting up one of the big signs Shawna's mother had lettered, and Melissa was untangling a strand of neon-orange plastic pennants near the entrance to the lot, next to the other sign.

"What's going on?" Shawna asked Gene.

"I told you the guys were going to give us a hand," he replied.

"Where'd you get all the lights and the pennants?"

"Kenny. His dad used to manage a car lot."

Shawna glanced up to the flat roof. Kenny smiled shyly down at her. She waved, then hastily backed out of Gene's way as he repositioned his stepladder.

"Did Chuck tell you what it's going to cost to have the power turned on?" Shawna asked.

"No problem," Gene said cheerfully. "We came up with an alternative plan. We're going to trade greens for electricity. Tell her, Melissa."

"I talked it over with Mom, and she said it'd be all right for you to run some cords to the store and use our power," said Melissa.

"In exchange, we're going to share our pine boughs," Gene added.

Shawna knew it was childish to feel miffed because she hadn't been consulted, especially when it was such a good idea. They got what they needed, and Melissa got what she wanted. *Doesn't she always?* Shawna thought.

"Actually, Shawna, I was thinking you and I could work together on the wreaths," Melissa said brightly. "I can supply ribbons and dried flowers and all the trimmings. We can sell them in Mom's shop and here, too. And we can split the profits right down the middle."

Shawna noticed Chuck watching her, an uneasy expression on his face. Was he worried that she'd turn Melissa down? She felt embarrassed that her feelings about Melissa were so obvious.

Melissa's voice interrupted Shawna's thoughts. "The workroom in back of the shop is small and awfully crowded, but the guys said they'd set up some tables for us here in the service garage. That should give us plenty of room to work. What do you say, Shawna? Can we be partners?"

Under any other circumstances, Melissa was the last person Shawna would have picked as a partner. But the pressure was on. Chuck, Gene, and half the basketball team were watching her. She couldn't possibly say no. Besides, it didn't make good business sense.

"Okay," Shawna said at last. "You've got a deal. If I find the time, we can start working on the wreaths tomorrow."

Chuck was beaming now. "That's what I started to tell you in the store. This all came up kind of suddenly—I figured you'd want to have some input."

Yeah, right, Shawna thought glumly. With

her sugary sweet act, Melissa was worming her way in—and Shawna was powerless to stop her.

But with Gene's friends around, it was impossible to remain glum for long. They ran around and worked like crazy. Jimmy and Kenny helped Melissa string up the pennants which flapped smartly in the breeze, drawing attention to Season's Greetings. Gene, Brandon, and Chuck finished hooking up the electric lights and turned them on just as the sun went down. The guys unwrapped the netting from the last of the trees and measured them while Shawna tied on the appropriate color-coded tags.

"Hey, Shawna! Was that really you on the radio this afternoon?" Jimmy asked, passing her a blue tag.

"Shh!" Shawna hissed, but not in time.

Gene's eyebrows drew together. "*You* were on the radio? What for?"

"She called the WXBN audience participation line and offered them a free tree," Melissa said, giggling.

"What's so funny?" asked Gene. "Don't tell me. Squirt said something stupid, right?"

"No she didn't. She did just fine." Chuck put one arm around Shawna's shoulders and gave her a reassuring squeeze.

"The guy on the other end was the stupid one," Jimmy said. "He just didn't get it."

"Guess you can hold off on those adoption

papers," Shawna whispered, appreciating Chuck's defense. He grinned as he withdrew his arm.

Now that the sun had set, the air grew colder. One of the guys suggested building a fire. They collected a pile of wood, and Jimmy set it ablaze while Kenny went to the nearest grocery store for hot dogs and marshmallows.

Melissa's mother closed her shop and stopped by to say hello. Shawna hoped she'd take Melissa with her when she left. But no such luck.

On impulse, Shawna went across the street to the Red Caboose and called Courtney.

"Brandon's here and some of the other guys," she said. "Melissa, too." The tone of her voice indicated her feelings on that subject.

"What about Brewster?" asked Courtney.

"Nowhere to be seen. Their study date must not have gone well. Better get over here before she starts 'studying' Brandon."

"I'll be right there!" Courtney announced.

"And bring some hot-dog sticks. This has turned into a cookout," Shawna said before she hung up.

Courtney did even better. She brought chips, homemade cookies, and enough soda for everyone. They sat around the fire on crates, barrels, and whatever else they could find. A couple of prospective customers dropped in, and Shawna jumped up to wait on them. When she returned, Kenny passed her a roasted hot dog.

"I burned it a little," he said apologetically.

"That's okay. I like them well-done," Shawna assured him, smiling.

Kenny smiled, too, and sat down next to her on an empty oil barrel. His shyness quickly disappeared, and soon he was toasting marshmallows and feeding them to Shawna one by one.

Shawna glanced up to find Chuck watching them from across the fire. The flames didn't provide enough light for her to read his expression, but Shawna was sure she knew what he was thinking. She hoped he wasn't going to tease her about Kenny. Melissa, who had been flitting around from guy to guy, snuggled down next to Chuck. A moment later they were sharing a roasting stick and laughing as they stuffed themselves with marshmallows.

Shawna turned on the radio in the office, and everyone began singing along to the Christmas tune that was playing.

Passing cars slowed and some of them even stopped to listen to all the music.

In the midst of all the fun, Shawna, Gene, and Chuck sold more trees than they'd sold all day. The evening passed quickly. At nine, when the group broke up, Shawna heard

Chuck offer Melissa a ride home, and naturally, she accepted. Gene got into Heck's car, and Courtney took off with Brandon.

Chuck turned to Shawna. "What about you, Half-Pint? Need a lift?"

"I'll drop her off," Kenny offered before Shawna could reply. She didn't really have a choice, so she followed him to his car.

"Heat's coming. You'll warm up in a minute," Kenny promised.

Shawna's eyes followed Chuck as he helped Melissa get into his truck, then climbed in himself. Jimmy and another guy got in, too, pushing Melissa right against Chuck.

Shawna tried to be good company on the short ride home, but when Kenny left her at her door, she hadn't the faintest recollection of their conversation. She went straight upstairs and filled the tub with hot water. The bubble bath certainly soothed her aching muscles, but nothing could cure her aching heart.

After she got into bed, Shawna lay awake a long time. Kenny was sweet. Did he have a crush on her? Shawna liked him as a friend, but as a boyfriend . . . he didn't make her tingle all over the way Chuck did.

Chuck. She whispered his name aloud. Had he taken Jimmy and the other boy home first? Had Melissa stayed snuggled next to him when the other two were gone?

Had he asked Melissa to the dance? Held her hand? Kissed her?

Today at Mahogany's for one glorious moment, Shawna had thought that Chuck was noticing her in a new way. But she must have been mistaken. She buried her head beneath the pillow and shut her eyes tight, trying to force sleep to come.

Chapter Ten

On Saturday morning, Shawna spent more time than usual fussing with her hair and makeup. She brushed and curled her hair until it gleamed, then experimented with eye shadow, blending a soft gray-blue with a violet tint. She applied mascara, pink lip-gloss, and added a touch of blush to her cheeks. Glancing in the mirror, she felt quite pleased with the effect.

Out in the driveway, a horn honked. Startled, Shawna flew to the window. Chuck was early! She hastily tugged on wool pants and a matching deep purple sweater over her long johns. She pulled on her best black boots just as the doorbell chimed.

Shawna rushed downstairs and grabbed

her coat and gloves. Her parents were in the kitchen, and Gene was still asleep. "I'll get it," she called, and ran to open the front door.

"Come on in, Chuck," she said, breathlessly.

He was wearing faded jeans, an army surplus jacket, worn sneakers, and a dark knitted cap. He stared at her in surprise. "I thought you and Melissa were going to make wreaths this morning."

Shawna nodded. "That's right."

"But you're all dressed up."

"No, I'm not. It's an old outfit." Out of the corner of her eye, Shawna saw her mother standing in the kitchen doorway, looking startled. She had been with Shawna when she bought the slacks and sweater just a few weeks before.

Shawna quickly took the thermos of hot chocolate her mother was holding, gave her a kiss on the cheek, and waved to her father. "Let's go!" she said to Chuck.

For some reason, the conversation between them was strained, unlike their normal easy banter. Shawna was glad to find a customer waiting when they arrived at Season's Greetings. Making a sale and tying the tree to the woman's car bridged the tension between her and Chuck.

"Last night was fun," Chuck said as he put the money from the sale into their cash box.

"But what about Heck's singing?" he grimaced. "With a voice like that, he should be jailed for noise pollution."

Shawna laughed. "I'll tell you who surprised me—Kenny. He has a beautiful voice. Of course, he sang so softly you had to be right beside him to hear."

Chuck's eyebrows raised. "What other hidden talents does Kenny have that I should know about?"

It was the sort of teasing Shawna had been expecting. "I might ask you the same thing about Melissa," she countered.

"You know Melissa—subtlety isn't her thing."

"And what is?" Shawna asked, uncertain what to make of his response.

He grinned. "As far as you're concerned, you'd better hope it's making wreaths. She's pretty excited about it. Which reminds me, I'm supposed to pick up a couple of tables from her house. She wants to set them up in the service garage so the two of you can work there."

Shawna wrinkled her nose. "To tell you the truth, I'm not sure I'll be much good at making wreaths."

"Melissa can show you. I'm sure you'll catch on quickly."

The idea of having to learn anything from Melissa annoyed Shawna, but a deal was a deal. Chuck put a kerosene heater in the service garage, and drove off to get the tables.

Shawna wasn't surprised when Melissa, as lovely as ever in a russet sweater almost the color of her hair, returned with him. Since sales were slow, she had no excuse to delay working on the wreaths. So with Chuck's help she began carrying in the discarded pine boughs while Melissa ran next door to get the other supplies they'd need.

The morning seemed endless to Shawna. Though the heater had taken some of the chill out of the garage, her feet were freezing in her unlined boots, and her cold fingers seemed almost numb. Melissa didn't seem to mind the cold at all. Her hands flew as fast as her tongue. She talked about school, guys, her mother's shop, and the Christmas dance as wreath after wreath took shape.

"I understand you've already bought your dress," Melissa said, deftly tying a bright ribbon into a bow.

Shawna looked at her in surprise. "Who told you that?"

"Chuck. He said you went shopping yesterday." Melissa tucked some baby's breath into the bow. "Where did you get your dress? What color is it?"

"I bought it at Mahogany's, and it's deep purple." Shawna knew if she didn't change the subject fast, Melissa would ask who was taking her to the dance. Pretending to burn herself, she dropped the glue gun. "Ouch! That thing's hot!"

"Be careful!" Melissa said. She added a cluster of cinnamon sticks to her ribbon arrangement. "Brewster wants me to go to the dance with him," she continued, not distracted by Shawna's ploy. "He's okay, but . . . well, he's just no *challenge*, if you know what I mean."

"Then you told him no?"

"Not exactly. I mean, what if no one else asks me?"

"In other words, you're waiting to see if you get a better offer?" Shawna said dryly.

"You got it!" Melissa exclaimed, oblivious to Shawna's sarcasm.

Staring down at the greens she was struggling with, Shawna hesitated for a second and then couldn't help asking, "Well, who do you *want* to go with?"

"I haven't decided for sure. I've got my eye on a couple of guys." Melissa fastened the bow to her wreath. "Does Gene have a date yet?"

Relieved, Shawna shook her head. "So far I don't think he's asked anyone."

Melissa giggled. "I've got a real weakness for basketball players. But I'll tell you who else I think is cute, who isn't on the team, and that's Chuck. What about you? Who are you going with?"

Before Shawna could figure out how to

reply, the door leading from the office opened, and in walked Chuck.

"How are you doing?" he asked the girls.

Shawna studied her one finished wreath. It looked pathetic beside the three beauties Melissa had so effortlessly created.

"I'm pretty hopeless at this," she said.

"I didn't want to say anything, but now that you mention it. . . ." Melissa giggled. "The greenery is nice and full," she added tactfully. "It's just a little plain, that's all. It needs something besides pine boughs and a red ribbon. But, don't give up—you'll get the hang of it after a while."

Just then Gene came stomping in. He had a game coming up that night, and he was full of nervous energy. He wandered out to the sales lot and back again. Plunking down on a barrel, he glanced at his watch. "It's noon. Anyone hungry besides me?"

"I'm starved," Melissa chimed in. "Let's go over to the Red Caboose and grab a bite."

"Good idea." Gene took her arm. At the door, he turned back and called out, "You coming, Chuck?"

Chuck shook his head. "No thanks. I'll eat later."

"If you're worried about missing a customer, little sister can tend to business. She doesn't mind, do you, Squirt?" Gene said.

"Of course not," Shawna fibbed brightly. "Go ahead, Chuck. I can manage here."

Chuck followed Gene and Melissa across the street.

As Shawna waited on the few customers who came by, Melissa's breezy confession rang in her ears. If Melissa decided to pursue Chuck, what chance did Shawna have? No chance at all. Her spirits dropped lower and lower.

Snow was beginning to fall when a familiar figure came loping across the lot. "Hi, Shawna. How's business?" Kenny asked, coming into the office where Shawna was warming up. He wiped a few big, wet snowflakes off his glasses.

"It wasn't bad this morning. But it's kind of slow right now." Remembering her thermos of cocoa, she poured some for herself and Kenny.

"Are you the only one here?" he asked, sipping his hot drink.

"Gene and Chuck are at the Red Caboose, eating lunch. Melissa went with them."

"Melissa's been here, too?"

Shawna nodded. "All morning. We've been making wreaths. Want to see?" She led the way into the service garage.

"Which ones did you make?" he asked.

Reluctantly, Shawna pointed to her scraggly effort.

"How much do you want for it?"

Shawna made a face. "Sad as it looks, I'd be lucky if I could *give* it away."

Kenny took out his wallet, grinning. "Name your price, Shawna. I'm going to buy it for my grandmother."

"Oh, don't be silly. Take one of Melissa's," Shawna urged. "They're much prettier."

"Gram doesn't care for a lot of fussy frills. She'll like yours best. Come on. How much?"

Shawna shrugged and named a price. She was putting money in the cash box when the boys and Melissa tramped in.

Melissa shook the snow out of her long hair. "Kenny!" she cried, realizing what had just happened. "Don't tell me you've bought Shawna's wreath instead of one of mine! You really hurt my feelings," she added with a pretty pout.

Kenny turned six shades of red. "It's for my grandmother. But I could buy one of yours for my mother," he finally managed to blurt.

Melissa laughed. "Oh, that's okay. I was only kidding."

Looking thoroughly uncomfortable, Kenny picked up his wreath and started to head for the door. Then he turned back and asked, "are you going to the game tonight?"

"Who, me?" Shawna murmured since he seemed to be looking at her.

"I wouldn't miss it for the world," Melissa said loudly. "How about you, Chuck?"

"I hate to miss it, but I'd better stay here."

"Me, too," Shawna said quickly. "It's

Saturday night, and a lot of people will be out shopping. Business should be booming."

Kenny looked as if he were having a hard time making up his mind about something. Finally, he said all in a rush, "If you can get away for a few hours tomorrow afternoon, maybe we could go roller-skating. The new rink out on Route Twelve is having its grand opening."

"Who, me?" a startled Shawna said for a second time.

Melissa giggled. "Who else, silly?"

Kenny flushed and nodded. "That is if you want to."

"Go ahead, Squirt. Chuck and I can run this place without you," Gene said.

Shawna could think of no way to turn Kenny down without thoroughly embarrassing him, so she smiled and accepted. "Courtney just learned to skate," she added, thinking fast. "Maybe she and Brandon would like to double."

"Fine by me," Kenny agreed. "I'll call you later for details, okay, Shawna?"

Shawna said it was, and Kenny left, carrying the wreath she had made.

That afternoon they sold quite a few trees, and by five o'clock, Shawna's black boots were soaked. Hungry and freezing, she agreed when Chuck urged her to go home with Gene.

"If I can't handle this alone, I'll just run across the street and give you a call," Chuck promised.

As soon as they got home, Shawna took a long, hot bath and ate dinner with her family. After Gene left for the game, she called Courtney about doubling the next afternoon on her roller-skating date. Courtney thought it sounded like fun, but she couldn't talk long because she had to go cheer at the game.

Shawna's parents tried to talk her into going with them to see Gene play, but the possibility of Chuck calling, needing her help, made her decline.

Once they'd gone, the house seemed very quiet. As tired as she was, Shawna sat by the phone, hoping Chuck would call. But when the phone finally rang, it was Kenny.

"I thought you were at the game," Shawna said.

"I am. It's halftime."

"Who's winning?"

"We are. But that's not why I called. I want to talk about tomorrow," Kenny explained.

Shawna told him that Courtney and Brandon were joining them. "We can meet them at the rink around two," she added.

"Great! I'll pick you up at one forty-five," Kenny said. "I'd better go now. The second half is about to begin."

*   *   *

102

The next morning Shawna dressed in her favorite jeans, a long, full orange blouse, and a leather vest composed mostly of fringe and beads. She tied her hair back with a leather thong and used very little makeup.

Kenny picked her up right on time. He was so shy that the conversation at first was awkward. But once Courtney and Brandon joined them, he loosened up a bit.

Kenny turned out to be an excellent skater, as was Courtney. Shawna could at least stay on her feet. But poor Brandon, a vision of skill and grace on the basketball court, couldn't seem to keep his skates beneath him on the roller rink.

"Brandon, you're an embarrassment," Courtney teased, helping him up for at least the tenth time.

"Maybe we should take a break," Kenny suggested.

"Let's get a bite to eat," Courtney said.

"Better do it right now, while I've still got a few teeth left for chewing," Brandon added, and everyone laughed.

Kenny took Shawna's hand as they left the rink and headed for the refreshment stand. They listened to the music and chatted over sodas and hot pretzels, then returned to the rink for another hour of skating.

On the way home, Kenny drove past Season's Greetings, but Chuck and Gene had closed it down for the day. It was easy to see why—the street was almost deserted.

"Guess I get the night off," Shawna said.

"If you're not in a hurry to get home—" Kenny began.

Shawna cut him short. "I've had a lovely time, Kenny. But school starts again tomorrow, so I better use the evening for homework. Thanks anyway."

"Thanks for coming." Kenny glanced over at her for an instant and smiled. "I know you'd just as soon have spent the afternoon selling trees with Chuck."

Blushing, Shawna started to protest, but Kenny brushed it aside. "Hey, it's okay. Your secret's safe with me."

"How did you know?" Shawna mumbled.

"About Chuck? I've seen the way you look at him."

Shawna winced. "I didn't know it was so obvious. I hope I didn't give you the wrong idea—about you and me, I mean."

"Relax, I'm fine. In fact, as long as we're being honest, I should tell you I've got a pretty big crush on someone, too. Trouble is, she doesn't know I'm alive."

"Who is she?" Shawna blurted out, surprised.

Kenny grinned. "If you have to ask, then I guess I'm doing a pretty good job of hiding it."

He dropped her at her door, and as Shawna went inside, she ran over a list of names in her mind, trying to figure out who Kenny liked. At least he could have given her one little clue!

Chapter Eleven

Shawna's Business Economics class on Monday began a unit on small businesses. Each student was to pick a partner, and together they were to pretend they were establishing their own business. They had to develop an overall plan on paper, and at the end of the unit, they would write a term paper, including charts, graphs, and other supplementary material.

Shawna told Courtney all about it on the ride home from school. "Now here's an assignment that I can really sink my teeth into!" she said.

"I'll bet you're the only one who actually has established a business," Courtney said. "Have you picked your partner yet?"

Shawna nodded. "Kenny and I are going to work on it together."

Courtney grinned and shot her a sidelong glance. "Hmm."

Shawna flushed. "We're just friends."

"Really? It looked like you two were getting along pretty well at the skating rink yesterday."

"Friends are *supposed* to get along," Shawna said. "Anyway, I can't seem to give up on Chuck. And Kenny likes someone else, too."

"Who?" Courtney asked eagerly.

"I don't know. He wouldn't say." Shawna unsnapped her seat belt and prepared to get out of the car. "Would you mind waiting while I change clothes? I could use a ride to Season's Greetings. Gene's got practice, and I don't want Chuck to be there all alone."

"I'll bet you don't!" Courtney said knowingly. They both laughed.

Business slowed down around six, but it picked up after the dinner hour until about eight. That pattern repeated itself all week and the next one.

As Christmas drew nearer, snowy, blustery days were followed by stinging cold nights. The office was as drafty as the service garage, and Shawna piled on several layers of sweatshirts and sweaters just to stay comfortable.

But neither cool air nor Shawna's cool attitude discouraged Melissa from coming by every night. If Shawna was too busy to help make wreaths, Melissa amused herself flirting with Chuck. When Gene came after basketball practice, she flirted with him, too.

"They've always been such good friends. I'd hate to see Melissa come between them," Shawna complained to Courtney at lunch one day.

"If those two aren't smarter than that, they deserve what they get," said Courtney.

Shawna remembered Courtney's words later that afternoon. Chuck was on the sales lot, and Gene, who had a game that evening, was free to help after school for a change. He was trying to squeeze a six-foot tree into a woman's compact car. Kenny was in the office working with Shawna on their project for Business Economics.

Melissa stuck her head into the office. "A light bulb just burned out. Are there any spares?"

"Not that I know of." Shawna glanced up from her textbook to see Melissa flash her dimples at Kenny.

"Kenny, there's at least a *foot* of snow out there, and I didn't wear my boots. Do you suppose you could go next door and ask my mother for a light bulb?" Melissa asked, batting her eyelashes.

Kenny bolted off his stool, and grabbed his coat. "No problem!"

Melissa fluttered her lashes at him. "Thank you, you sweet thing!"

Kenny's ears turned brighter red than the bow on the office door. As he dashed out, Shawna glowered at Melissa. "Kenny has to keep stats for the game later, so we don't have much time to study. I'd really appreciate it if you'd run your own errands."

"Oh, it'll only take him a second," Melissa said.

Just then, Chuck came in, followed by a woman and three little kids. While the woman was paying for her tree, Kenny returned, light bulb in hand, followed by Gene.

Melissa thanked Kenny and disappeared into the service garage with the bulb. "I can't reach the receptacle," she called out a moment later. "What I need is a nice, tall basketball player to help me. Or, if he's too busy, I'd settle for a clever Christmas-tree salesman."

Shawna stepped back to avoid the stampede as Chuck, Gene, and Kenny all dashed to Melissa's aid. Shawna muttered to herself, "How many morons does it take to change a light bulb?"

Chuck stuck his head back into the office. "Were you talking to me, Half-Pint?"

"No, just telling myself a joke," Shawna replied, scowling.

An hour later, Gene, Kenny, and Melissa all left for the game. Shawna knew Chuck enjoyed basketball, so she said, "I can handle this alone, if you'd like to go, too. The Rockets are playing the West Central Demons. Gene thinks it'll be a close one."

"Thanks, but I'd rather stay here and rake in the dough. Why don't you go, though?"

"I don't really *like* basketball that much," Shawna confessed. "And as for 'raking it in,' that may be a slight exaggeration."

"Business is picking up now that it's getting closer to Christmas," Chuck pointed out. "I think those advertising gimmicks you and Kenny came up with last week helped, too."

"Tips straight out of our Business Economics textbook. It's amazing what you learn in school," Shawna joked.

"How are you and Kenny coming along on your project, anyway?" Chuck asked.

"We've gotten pretty good grades on the papers we've turned in so far. I suppose they could have been better, but between Kenny's part-time job and my spending so much time here, we haven't been able to put as many hours into it as we might have otherwise."

"Not to mention your fast-food dates."

Shawna was surprised by his tone. "A trip to Biggies isn't a date. I mean, we *do* have to eat sometimes. Since when do you care where Kenny and I go, anyway?"

Chuck turned away abruptly and wandered to the window. "Just skip it, okay?

Speaking of eating, I'm hungry. How does pizza sound to you? My treat."

"In that case, it sounds great," Shawna said, aware that he'd neatly avoided answering her question.

"Run over to Mrs. Doty's and call it in then, while I wait on this customer."

Business had slowed to a trickle by the time the delivery man arrived with their pizza. He was shivering as he came through the door.

"It's snowing like crazy, and the wind is really whipping the power lines around. The roads are getting treacherous, too. You kids should probably close up and go home," he said. Chuck paid him for the pizza, and he went back out into the storm.

"What do you think, Chuck? Should we close?" Shawna asked.

"Let's give it half an hour. If we don't sell any more trees, we'll go home."

Chuck pushed the big crate Shawna had been using as a desk closer to the heater. "Come on—let's eat."

Shawna poured two cups of steaming hot apple cider from her thermos and passed one to Chuck. When Chuck opened the pizza box, the delicious aroma filled the small office. Shawna suddenly felt very snug and content. The thick crust was just the way she liked it, and she reached for a second piece.

111

"Me, too, please." Chuck grinned and held out his napkin.

They munched in comfortable silence. Chuck finally broke it. "Are you ever going to tell me your joke?"

Shawna lowered her gaze. "You wouldn't think it was funny."

"Try me," he insisted, his dark eyes dancing. "I've got a pretty good sense of humor."

Shawna gave in. "Okay. How many morons does it take to change a light bulb?"

"I don't know. How many?"

"Never mind—it isn't funny anymore. Come to think of it, it wasn't very funny to start with," Shawna said, suddenly losing her courage.

Chuck looked at her closely for a long moment. "This wouldn't have anything to do with that burned-out bulb in the service garage, would it? Or how fast Kenny jumped in to help Melissa?"

Her eyes widened. "*Kenny?* As I recall—"

"Oh, go on and admit it," he interrupted, grinning. "Melissa flirted with your boyfriend, and you got mad."

"Kenny *isn't* my boyfriend!" Shawna snapped.

Chuck looked skeptical. "Then why are you having such a hard time being nice to Melissa?"

"I don't like how she treats you guys, okay?" Shawna bit into her piece of pizza and chewed furiously. "She plays one against the other. She rolls her eyes and flutters her lashes and giggles and teases until you're falling all over her. She just loves seeing all three of you dance to her tune!"

To Shawna's surprise, Chuck laughed. "Don't you think I know that?"

"Then why do you fall for it?" she demanded.

Chuck shrugged. "The old competitive streak, I guess. It's sort of like a game. What I want to know is, why does it make you so mad?"

"Never mind. I'm going home." Shawna leapt up, pulled on her jacket, and flung open the door. Chuck followed her, grabbing her arm.

"What are you—nuts? It's practically a blizzard out there!" he said. "If you really want to leave, I'll close up and drive you home."

"Don't bother, I'll walk!"

"That temper of yours is going to get you in trouble someday," he warned, trying not to laugh. But when he saw her serious face, his amused expression faded. "I'm sorry, Half-Pint. I shouldn't have teased you about Melissa and Kenny," he said gently. "I didn't mean to make you mad. It's just that you're usually such a good-natured kid." Smiling, he added, "Forgive me?"

113

"Chuck, once and for all, I'm *not* a kid! And while we're on the subject, I wish you'd quit calling me Half-Pint. I have a *name*!"

Chuck looked confused. "But I've always called you Half-Pint."

"I didn't care when I *was* a kid. But I'm not anymore, and now I *do* care. Things have changed, in case you haven't noticed," Shawna said angrily.

He gave her a long, steady look. His expression was difficult to read. Shawna's heart was beating so fast that she felt short of breath.

"I guess things *have* changed, haven't they? Seeing you at the dress shop the other day . . . and then with Kenny . . . yes, things sure have changed," Chuck said at last.

Shawna murmured, "I'd just like it a lot better if you—and Gene, too—would stop treating me like I'm still a child."

"Fair enough," he said softly. "Now, if this argument is over, let's kiss and make up, okay?" He bent his head and brushed her lips with his in a quick kiss. It was just a token of friendship, nothing more, but Shawna felt as if she might actually faint.

Smiling into her astonished face, Chuck wrapped an arm around her shoulders and turned her around, saying, "Let's shut the door before we both freeze to death."

And then the lights went out.

Chapter Twelve

"The wind must have brought down a major power line," Chuck said, peering out the window. "Looks like it shut off everything downtown."

"We may as well go home, then," said Shawna.

Chuck put on his coat, hat, and gloves, Shawna picked up the cash box, and they stepped out into the storm. A snowplow rattled past on the deserted street.

"He's fighting a losing battle." Away from the windbreak of the building, Chuck's words were nearly lost in the howling wind. Drifts of snow were forming across the lot. *The pizza delivery man was right*, Shawna thought as she climbed into the truck. *We should have started home sooner.* She sat shivering as Chuck warmed up the engine.

Neither spoke much on the trip home. The darkness blanketing the city made everything seem eerie, and Shawna's heart squeezed tight as Chuck concentrated on driving through the blowing snow. "Don't worry. It'll be all right," he said, sensing her fear.

Half an hour later, they arrived at Shawna's house, safe and sound. The porch light was burning brightly, so obviously the power outage hadn't affected her neighborhood. "Call me. That way, I'll know you got home okay," Shawna said as she got out of the truck.

"I didn't know you cared," Chuck joked.

Blushing, Shawna couldn't think of a thing to say.

Shawna hadn't been home long when her parents and Gene returned from the game.

"Who won?" she asked.

"The lights went out so they had to call it," her father told her.

"Wouldn't you know it? I was playing my best game of the season!" Gene grumbled.

"In whose opinion?" Shawna teased.

Gene just scowled at her and stalked off to his room, slamming his door.

"What's his problem?" Shawna asked.

"His ego's a little bruised, I'm afraid. Be-

116

fore the game, he asked Melissa Doty to the holiday dance. She turned him down," Mrs. Cayley explained.

"You're kidding! Not very long ago, Melissa was telling me how cute she thought he was!"

Mr. Cayley shook his head in mock dismay. "You women sure give us men a rough time. How did you get home, honey? We were worried about you."

"Chuck drove me," Shawna replied.

Her mother smiled at her father. "I told you that Shawna was in good hands."

Good arms, too, Shawna thought with a sigh. *Good everything.* She said good night to her parents, then went upstairs. While she was in the bathtub, she heard the phone ring. A moment later, her mother knocked on the door.

"That was Chuck, letting you know he made it home safely."

Shawna started to get out of the tub. "I forgot he was going to call! Tell him to wait a second—I'll be right there."

"Honey, he already hung up," her mother said.

Disappointed, Shawna sank farther into the water. She closed her eyes and savored the memory of Chuck's lips brushing hers. Even though it had been a very casual kiss, it *had* to mean he realized she wasn't a little kid anymore. And maybe, just maybe there was still a slight chance that he'd invite her to the dance.

Chuck pulled up in front of Shawna's house midmorning with a snow blade attached to the front of his truck. While he was plowing the driveway, Shawna flung on her warmest clothes and grabbed a bite of breakfast. Last night's kiss had made her feel a little shy with Chuck, so she was glad when Gene went with them to Season's Greetings.

Traffic was moving again on Main Street, but her first glimpse of the lot filled Shawna with dismay. The trees were almost buried in snow, and their branches drooped under its weight. The drifts were enormous. *How will we ever dig out of this mess?* Shawna wondered. Before they could decide where to start, a young boy in a tattered coat and mismatched mittens waded through the snow toward them.

"Are the trees no good now?" he asked.

"I think they'll be all right," Shawna said as Chuck went to work with the snow blade.

"There might be some broken ones, though," said the boy.

"I'm hoping they'll be okay if we shake the snow off them right away."

The boy's eyes filled with a look of disappointment, and slowly he trudged away down the street.

Just then Melissa came out of her mother's shop. "Mom and I brought hot drinks and some sandwiches. Come on over when you need to warm up," she called.

"I'd rather freeze to death! Here, Squirt. Let's get this job done," Gene muttered, handing Shawna a shovel.

Poor Gene, Shawna thought. *He isn't used to rejection.*

After Chuck had moved as much snow as he could with his blade, he parked the truck and grabbed another shovel. Soon Kenny came along and pitched in. They all worked nonstop until noon, when Chuck and Kenny accepted Melissa's invitation to Doty's Dabblings. Gene refused to go, so Shawna went with him to the Red Caboose for soup and sandwiches. He didn't have much to say, but at least he'd stopped snapping at her.

By late afternoon, Shawna was worn out. Kenny suggested they go next door for another hot drink, and since Gene and Chuck were anxious to finish clearing the lot, Shawna and Kenny went alone. On their way into the shop, Shawna noticed the boy she'd seen earlier coming out of a side door.

"Who is that little kid?" she asked Melissa a moment later.

"Oh, that's Stephen," Melissa said, passing her a cup of steaming cocoa. She poured another for Kenny. "He and his mom are moving upstairs."

119

"There's an apartment up there?"

"Nothing fancy. But they needed something with a cheap rent, I guess," Melissa said with a shrug. Then she turned all her attention to Kenny. "A big, strong guy like you needs something to eat after all that shoveling. There's a plate of Christmas cookies in the back room. Why don't you go get them?"

Kenny's ears flamed. He stumbled over a basket on his way out, knocking his glasses askew. He was barely out of earshot when Melissa giggled and said to Shawna, "You know what? He'd be cute if it wasn't for those dorky glasses. But never mind Kenny. I've got really exciting news!" She rolled her eyes dramatically. "Guess who's taking me to the dance?"

"I don't know. Who?" Shawna said warily.

Melissa smiled broadly. "Chuck!"

Shawna almost choked on her hot chocolate. "That's—nice," she managed to say, trying to hide her feelings. She felt her heart drop and as she lowered her head, she blinked back the hot tears welling up in her eyes. Melissa rattled on about what she intended to wear, how she was going to fix her hair, and what kind of flowers she wanted.

When the stream of chatter stopped, Shawna glanced up to find Melissa's eyes on her. "So who are you going with?"

Waves of heat flooded Shawna's face. How could she admit that she had no date?

"Well?" said Melissa eagerly. "Who is it?"

"She's going with me. Who'd you think?" Kenny said, coming over to Shawna. It seemed to her for an instant as if her misery was mirrored in his eyes, but she was too upset to wonder why.

He extended a hand. "Come on, Shawna. Let's get back to work."

Gratefully, Shawna clutched his warm hand. She clung to it as they walked through the store and out to the street. "Thanks, Kenny," she whispered, still fighting back tears.

"Are you kidding?" His smile was a little forced. "I'll be dancing with the prettiest girl there."

"Oh, no," Shawna said quickly. "I don't want you to feel like you *have* to take me to the dance. Saving me from total embarrassment in front of Melissa was enough."

"I know I don't have to. But I *want* to," Kenny insisted. "I mean it, Shawna." He sounded sincere, even grimly determined.

Shawna hesitated a moment, then squeezed his hand. "Okay, Kenny. It's a date!"

Never a graceful loser, Gene didn't take the news well when he found out that Chuck was taking Melissa to the dance. As far as Shawna knew, he never confronted Chuck about it, but from then on there was a tension between the two friends.

Shawna tried to be a better loser than Gene. But the hurt wouldn't easily go away. Whenever she and Chuck were working together, she felt uncomfortable and depressed. Apparently he was aware of it, because one evening at Season's Greetings he came right out and asked her if everything was all right.

Shawna pretended to be surprised. "Sure. Why do you ask?"

"I don't know. I thought maybe you were angry about something."

"Nope."

"You've been awfully quiet lately," he continued, looking puzzled. "You sure nothing's wrong?"

"I've got a lot on my mind. Oh, did I tell you guys I talked to the chairman of the dance committee yesterday?" Shawna said to Chuck and Gene, eager to change the subject. "I knew she was planning to buy trees for decorating, so it was a snap convincing her to buy them from us."

"Good for you, Half—uh, Shawna," Chuck replied.

"Maybe we should give them a discount. What do you think?"

"If it was me, I'd charge them full price,"

Gene muttered. "But I guess my opinion doesn't count for much. So you two do whatever you want." He glared in Chuck's direction, then stalked off to wait on a customer.

Shawna sighed. These days were so difficult that she actually began to look forward to the dance. Maybe when it was over, they could all go back to being friends. There didn't seem to be much else to hope for.

Chapter Thirteen

Shawna dropped a curtsy, congratulating herself. After a week of practice, she'd finally mastered walking in the gold high heels! She made one more graceful turn in front of the mirror, and stroked the lush velvet of her deep purple dress. Her hair, smoothly coiled at the nape of her neck, complemented the elegance of her dress. Shawna decided she looked very grown-up, and she was definitely three inches taller, thanks to the shoes.

A knock at her bedroom door interrupted her last-minute appraisal. She turned from the mirror, calling, "Come in."

"Kenny's here—" Gene stopped in his tracks and let out a low whistle. "Wow! You're looking pretty hot tonight, Squirt!"

"You don't look too bad yourself. You ought to wear a tux more often," Shawna replied, pleased.

"Play your cards right, and I might even ask you to dance." Gene extended his arm, and Shawna took it, laughing.

"I doubt Darla will let you out of her sight long enough to dance with me or anybody else!"

Just a few days ago, Darla Wilson had split up with her boyfriend. Darla was head cheerleader, and it was unthinkable for her to not have a date for the dance so she had asked Gene to take her.

Gene escorted Shawna downstairs where Kenny was waiting for her. When she saw him, Shawna blinked in surprise. The change in him went beyond his black tuxedo, plaid bow tie, and matching cummerbund. He'd gotten contacts! His hazel eyes, previously distorted by the thick lenses of his glasses, were gorgeous.

"You look really nice, Shawna," Kenny said shyly.

Shawna smiled. "Thanks, Kenny. So do you."

"These are for you." He gave her a florist box.

"Oh, how lovely!" Shawna exclaimed as she opened it. A cluster of tiny silver bells was the focal point of a wrist corsage of red sweetheart roses and baby's breath. Shawna slipped it on her wrist. Then Kenny helped her on with her cape. It had been her mother's when she was in college, and it was trimmed with white fur and lined in rich purple satin. The cape felt silky smooth against her bare shoulders.

They said good night to Mr. and Mrs. Cayley, and as they got into the car, Shawna couldn't help but notice how jittery Kenny seemed. "I'm a little nervous," Shawna admitted, trying to put him at ease.

He looked at her in surprise. "Really? Me, too. On the way to your house, I thought the shocks were bad in the car, but it was just me shaking," Kenny joked.

Shawna laughed. "My electric toothbrush was vibrating so much, I could hardly hang on to it. Then I realized it wasn't even turned on!"

For the rest of the drive, they made up "nervous" jokes. They were both relaxed and laughing when they entered the school. Kenny took Shawna's hand, leading her into the softly lighted, beautifully decorated gym.

"Nice trees," Shawna murmured, indicating the Christmas trees that lined the walls. They were decked in antique-style electric candles, silver garlands, and old-fashioned ornaments.

"Season's Greetings, huh?" Kenny said. When she nodded, he grinned. "You sure do have a head for business."

"But not tonight. Tonight, we dance," Shawna told him.

"I was right," Kenny said as they danced.

"About what?"

"There isn't a girl here who's half as pretty as you."

Shawna giggled "That's very sweet, but wait till the others arrive."

She fought the impulse to look around for Chuck and Melissa. Things were going so well—maybe if she gazed into Kenny's beautiful hazel eyes all evening, some magic chemistry would develop between them.

"Sharp threads, Kenny." George Heck tapped Kenny on the shoulder and winked at Shawna. "What do you say, man? Are you going to let me dance with your lady?"

Kenny grinned. "No way! Find your own girl."

"I came stag. Have some pity, will you?"

"Go ahead. Fight over me," Shawna said, laughing.

George pretended to be astonished. "Shawna? Is that really you? Well, I'll be!"

Shawna made a friendly swat at him, and he grabbed her hand.

"See, Kenny? She *does* want to dance with me!" With that, George waltzed Shawna right out of Kenny's arms.

After a few bars, the music changed to a funky rock beat. George grinned and swung

Shawna wide. "Now *this* is *real* dance music!" he exclaimed.

Shawna was out of breath by the time the song ended, and George escorted her back to Kenny. Almost immediately, Brewster asked her to dance. Jimmy Jones wanted a dance, too, and then Brandon cut in.

"Courtney's dancing with Kenny, so how about giving me a turn?" he asked.

When the number ended, they joined Kenny and Courtney by one of the refreshment tables. The two couples carried their snacks to a cozy candle-lit table in a corner. While they were eating, a photographer began setting up his equipment nearby.

"You kids want to go first?" he called to them.

Shawna felt a little self-conscious, posing with so many people around, but she did want a memento of the evening. The photographer positioned Kenny behind her and asked her to tilt her head slightly to the side. Out of the corner of her eye, Shawna could see the snowy backdrop screen. It reminded her of how the tree lot had looked the day after the storm, and of the night of the storm when Chuck had kissed her. She shifted her gaze, and her heart pounded as her eyes unexpectedly met Chuck's.

For a split second, everything else faded away. It seemed to Shawna as if the two of them were all alone in the room. Chuck had the strangest look on his face. He lifted his hand to wave and then the camera's flash went off.

Shawna tried to blink away the blinding bright spots before her eyes. When her vision cleared, she searched the room until she found Chuck again. He was dancing with Melissa, and Melissa had never looked more stunning. Her lovely red hair cascaded down her back almost to the waist of the formfitting white sequined dress she was wearing.

Shawna stood as if frozen, unable to look away. She couldn't believe anything could hurt so much as the sight of them dancing.

Kenny caught her cold hand in his. "Shawna?" he said gently. "Are you okay?"

She nodded, but of course she wasn't. The room suddenly felt too hot, too loud, too small. It was closing in on her, just like the car had in that strange dream she'd had a month or so ago.

"I think I need some air," she whispered.

Kenny took her arm and weaved his way through the crowd to the nearest door. "Are you sick?" he asked anxiously.

"No, I'm just . . ." To Shawna's embarrassment, one hot tear slid down her cheek. She almost ran the last few steps to the corridor. Fighting back the tears, she glanced up at Kenny.

To her surprise, he looked just as unhappy as she felt. And then all of a sudden everything fell into place. Of course! The girl Kenny had mentioned, the one who didn't know he was alive—it was Melissa!

For a moment, Shawna felt even sorrier for him than she felt for herself. At least she had the luxury of shedding a few tears.

"And we were having such a good time, too," she said very softly.

"We can go back in," Kenny said. "If you want to, that is."

"I think I'd like to go home. But Kenny, why don't you stay?"

He shook his head.

"No, listen," she said earnestly. "I *know* Melissa. If you'll listen and do what I say, you've got as good a chance as the next guy —maybe better!"

"Shawna, she's way out of my league," Kenny mumbled.

Shawna's eyes flashed. "She is not! You deserve ten times better. But I know how it is. Our hearts don't always listen to our heads. So here's my advice—ignore her. Act like you could care less whether she so much as glances your way."

Kenny looked skeptical. "Ignore her? Ignore *Melissa*? But she loves attention."

Shawna nodded. "That's exactly my point. She also loves a challenge. That's why she dumped Brewster and who knows how many others. They just fell at her feet. It was too easy."

At first, Kenny looked at her as if she were crazy. Then slowly he began to grin. "You just may have something there," he said finally. "Thanks, Shawna! But let me take you home, first."

She shook her head. "You go right back in. I'll call a cab. Go on, Kenny. And good luck," she added.

Fifteen minutes later, Shawna was in a cab on her way home. *Forget romance,* she thought gloomily. Kenny was right when he said she had a good head for business. So from now on, she'd forget about love and concentrate on dollars and *sense.*

Shawna glanced at the clock on the instrument panel. It was too early to go home. She knew her parents would ask a lot of questions that she didn't feel like answering yet. "I've changed my mind," she said to the driver, and gave him the address of Season's Greetings.

Chapter Fourteen

The door to the office was locked, and Shawna hadn't brought her key. But she knew where an extra one was hidden. She went around to the back of the building, picking her way through the snow. Her feet were freezing in the gold high heels. As she patted the underside of the windowsill in the dark, feeling for the key, she heard a voice call out. "Hey! What're you doing?"

Startled, Shawna swung around. The little boy who lived above Doty's Dabblings was standing a few yards away.

Relief washed over her. "You scared me!" she exclaimed.

"Oh, it's you! I thought someone was breaking in," he said. He trotted over to her.

"Every night I watch the place for you, just in case someone tries to steal a tree or something. There aren't many of them left, are there?"

"No. We'll probably sell out in the next couple of days."

The boy's face fell, and Shawna wondered for the first time if his mother had a tree. "Are you about ready for Christmas?" she asked as her icy fingers finally found the key.

"I still have to get my mom something," he replied.

Shawna came back to the front of the building and unlocked the door. The boy followed her inside. As she turned on the light, his eyes widened. "You look like a princess!" he said.

In spite of the misery in her heart, Shawna smiled at him. "I've been to a dance. What about you? What are you doing out so late?"

"I'm going to the Red Caboose. My mom waits tables there. It's just about time for her to get off work."

"And you're going to walk her home? That's sweet."

The boy stared down at his ragged sneakers for a moment. "I guess I better go," he said at last, and started slowly out the door.

"Wait a second!" Shawna called after him.

He turned back, his big blue eyes questioning. "Yeah?"

"You never said what you're going to get for your mom."

He shook his head. "I can't tell. She might think that I asked, and I'm not supposed to ask."

"All right then. Maybe I'll see you tomorrow," Shawna said, puzzled.

As he walked away, Shawna stared thoughtfully after him. Was it a tree? Was that what the boy wanted for his mother? She had no way of knowing for sure, but it seemed to make sense. And if that was what he wanted, then why shouldn't he have it?

A moment later, Shawna wished that she were dressed in her working clothes as she tugged at one tree, then another. She was looking for one with a nice, full shape. But even if she found the perfect tree, how was she ever going to drag it up to the apartment by herself?

"Shawna? What on earth are you doing here?"

She instantly recognized Chuck's deep voice. Astonished, she spun around to face him. "I'm picking out a tree for the little boy who lives over Mrs. Doty's shop." Shawna swallowed hard. "What are *you* doing here?"

"Looking for you. I saw the light, and I thought this was a good starting place."

"Wh—where's Melissa?" Shawna stammered.

"I asked Kenny to take over for me," Chuck said.

Shawna's mouth dropped open. "Why did you do that? I thought you were crazy about her."

"It's kind of complicated." Shivering, Chuck shoved his hands into his pockets. "If I promise to help you with the tree, do you suppose we could go inside and talk first?"

Shawna was trembling, too, but not from the cold. "Okay, talk," she said, looking up at Chuck when they were inside.

Clearly uncomfortable, he said, "Well, Melissa kept going on about how terrific Kenny looked without his glasses, like she was trying to make me jealous. I thought about what you said—you know, about her playing Gene and me against each other. That turned out pretty badly."

"You mean when Gene got mad because you asked her to the dance?"

"I *didn't* ask her, Shawna," Chuck said. "All I said was, 'Do you have a date for the dance?' and she said she didn't and she'd love to go with me. I felt kind of stuck, so I figured the only thing to do was take her. Pretty dumb, huh?"

Shawna said nothing, waiting for him to continue.

He hesitated a moment, avoiding her eyes. "Anyway," he said, "it caused a lot of trouble between Gene and me, but Melissa thought it was exciting. Then tonight I realized she was doing the same thing with Kenny and me—trying to play one against the other. That's when I handed her over to him."

Shawna thought how insulted Melissa would be if she found out that her date had actually wanted to get rid of her. But if anyone deserved it, Melissa did.

"I think she was glad to see me go," Chuck admitted. "Kenny didn't seem to mind, either."

"He's crazy about her," Shawna told him.

"Poor guy!" Chuck reached for her cold hand, squeezing it hard. "I wanted to go with you, Shawna. If Kenny hadn't asked you first—"

Shawna cut him off. "He didn't ask me until after you asked Melissa."

"But you bought your dress weeks ago. I figured he must have asked you then. If I'd known . . ." He looked puzzled.

Shawna could hardly believe what he was saying. Yet there he stood, looking at her the way she'd hoped and dreamed he might someday. Her pulse racing, she moved closer to him. "What are you thinking?" she asked in a low whisper.

"That I've been a real jerk," Chuck said with a wry smile. "I mean, we've been friends for such a long time, and somehow I guess I always thought love would happen first, then friendship. That's why I had such a hard time figuring out how I felt about you," Chuck struggled to explain. "But that day when I saw you in Mahogany's wearing this very dress . . ." The admiration in his dark eyes made Shawna quiver inside. "All at once, I realized that you'd grown up. I kicked myself all the way back here for letting some other guy steal you right out from under my nose."

"I kept telling you that Kenny and I were just friends," Shawna reminded him.

"Yeah, I know that now." He drew her even closer. "But never mind all that. Just tell me one thing."

"What?" Shawna asked breathlessly as he put his arms around her.

"When we kissed the night of the storm, did you feel what I felt?"

Shawna's lashes swept down, and a smile spread across her face.

"Really?" he said with a delighted grin, though she hadn't spoken a word. "The next day you acted so funny. I was afraid I'd made you mad or something."

"I thought *you* thought it was just a kiss between friends, to make up," she said.

Chuck rested his cheek on the top of her head. In a low voice, he replied, "It was a lot more than that. Believe me, Shawna, I was so happy." With one gentle finger, he tipped up her chin. His eyes searched her face, as if he were memorizing her features. Then slowly, he pressed his lips to hers.

The sweetness of his kiss warmed Shawna all over. As she put her arms around Chuck's neck, the bells on her wrist corsage jingled softly.

Chuck smiled down at her. "Am I hearing things, or did we just make bells ring?"

Laughing, Shawna kissed him again, wiggling her wrist. Chuck laughed, too, and hugged her tight. His arms felt so good around her!

"Now what were you doing out there on the lot?" he asked after a moment.

Shawna quickly explained about the tree. Hand in hand, they walked out onto the snowy lot in search of the perfect tree to brighten the little boy's Christmas. And there beneath a cold, starry sky, they shared another jingle-bell kiss.

Sweet Dreams

SWEET DREAMS are fresh, fun and exciting —alive with the flavor of the contemporary teen scene—the joy and doubt of first love. If you've missed any SWEET DREAMS titles, then you're missing out on your kind of stories, written about people like you!